George W. Heath

Southern Refugees

The South during the war - A military drama in five acts

George W. Heath

Southern Refugees
The South during the war - A military drama in five acts

ISBN/EAN: 9783337343767

Printed in Europe, USA, Canada, Australia, Japan

Cover: Foto ©Andreas Hilbeck / pixelio.de

More available books at **www.hansebooks.com**

Southern Refugees,

OR

HE SOUTH DURING THE WAR.

A Military Drama in Five Acts,

By Comrade GEO. W. HEATH,

(AUTHOR OF THE DRUMMER BOY OF THE SHENANDOAH.)

HAVERHILL, MASS., NOV. 22, 1872.

HAVERHILL:

WOODWARD & PALMER, PRINTERS.

1872.

CAST OF CHARACTERS.

—o—

UNION.

JARED WESTON,   CAPTAIN ALLEN,
FRED WESTON,   SERGEANT OF PICKET,
JAMES MOORE,   MR. MUTH,*
CATASTROPHY JACKSON,   MR. WATKINS,*
DOLPH,   MR. KENT,*
MAJ. GEN. COMMANDING,   MR. SMART.*
*Not Speaking parts.

LADIES.

MRS. WESTON,   ROSA ARRINGTON,
CARRIE WESTON,   GRACE HOLDEN,
MRS. ARRINGTON,   JERUSHA JENKINS.
GODDESSES OF LIBERTY, WAR, PEACE, HOPE, JUSTICE.
Staff Officers, Soldiers, Citizens, &c.

CONFEDERATES.

ROBERT WILLARD,   FRANK STARK,
HARRISON RATHBONE,   CAPTAIN WILSON,
GENERAL BUCKNER,   GEORGE BENNETT,
CHARLES CLAIRE.

Officers, Orderlies, Soldiers, Citizens, &c.

—०—

ACT I.

SCENE 1st. Room at Mrs. Arrington's. Yankee rule and Southern steel.

SCENE 2d. Garden at Mr. Weston's. Dolph in trouble; Jerusha's model for a husband; Catastrophy full of patriotism; " I'll die an old maid just to spite him."

SCENE 3d. Double Scene. Two rooms in a tavern at Brazoria; A Southern mob; the toast; " I do not know you or your cause"; friends in council; the lone star flag; the stars and stripes torn down; the oath; " I swear."

SCENE 4th. Wood. Catastrophy and Dolph on the lookout.

SCENE 5th. Street in Brazoria; the mob at the polls; " yeh votes here when yeh votes right;" the first blow; words and bullets.

SCENE 6th. Wood. The thunder storm and what was done in it; Catastrophy and Dolph put in an appearance; Rathbone in a tight place; Southern chivalry.

SCENE 7th. Room at Mr. Weston's. Dolph accepts the old rifle; his promise; father and son; the old man's advice; preparing for flight; the lock of hair and why it was treasured; a useful present; good-bye to home and friends; *Tableau—Union Refugees.*

ACT II.

SCENE 1st. Room at Mr. Weston's. Charges against Fred; the arrest; " May God protect us all ;" *Tableau—Hope beyond the Clouds.*

SCENE 2d. Wood. Jerusha's courage clear up; searching for a boat.

SCENE 3d. Bar-room in Smithland. Fred proposes a toast ; a terrible murder ; on the track ; appearance of Willard and Rathbone ; " away with them to prison."

SCENE 4th. Wood. Catastrophy and Jerusha again ; Willard and Rathbone on the trail ; " the wandering refugee" ; the blow in the dark ; tied up in a blanket ; " Ho, for the sunny south once more."

SCENE 5th. Pier scene by moonlight. Willard and Rathbone finish their work ; Fred thrown overboard ; the useful present saves a life ; Catastrophy and Jerusha take a boat ride ; what they saw in the water ; the rescue.

ACT III.

SCENE 1st. Village Landscape. Flag presentation ; off to the front.

SCENE 2d. Wood. "Halt ! who goes there?" taken prisoners.

SCENE 3d. Landscape. Union camp ; Catastrophy wants a uniform ; Jerusha's idea of politeness ; Dolph overjoyed ; " fall in."

SCENE 4th. Wood. Willard scouting.

SCENE 5th. Room scene. Union General's headquarters ; Fred detailed as a scout.

SCENE 6th. Wood. Foraging ; a small seizure.

SCENE 7th. Room scene. Rebel General's headquarters ; arrival of the mail ; Rathbone tells some startling news ; a new version of Fred's escape ; the story has an effect ; *Tableau— Homeless but not Friendless ;* " I'll take good care my enemies do not see them "

SCENE 8th. Wood. "String him up" ; Catastrophy's battalion to the rescue ; the tables turned.

SCENE 9th. Mountain Glen ; arrival of Fred with news ; the skirmish line falling back ; the battle ; capture of the field piece ; the fight for the flag ; wounded ; *Tableau—Our Banner Victorious.*

ACT IV.

SCENE 1st. Hospital scene. A faithful watcher ; brother and sister ; *Tableau—Some of those who saved us.*

SCENE 2d. Room in a hospital. Catastrophy anxious to return ; Jerusha objects ; she is overruled.

SCENE 3d. Wood. Scouting ; the captive ; arrival of Capt. Weston ; southern principles ; Fred's opinion of them.

Scene 4th. Landscape. Catastrophy on a spree; gobbled up; " rum and 'lasses."

Scene 5th. Rocky pass. Rebel camp; the tempting bottle; " don't you fear for me."

Scene 6th. Wood. Captured; a bragging lieutenant.

Scene 7th. Room scene. Rebel headquarters; Catastrophy before the Rebel General; what was found out by him; how the re-enforcements came; news of Vicksburg's surrender; the escape.

Scene 8th. Wood. The faithful sentinel; the assault; Union boys at hand.

ACT V.

Scene 1st. Southern Dungeon. Starving; the shot from the guard; an accursed record; a fearful wreck; the chords break; unconscious; waking; " Marching through Georgia"; death of Willard; *Tableau—The Final Roll Call.*

Scene 2d. Landscape. Going home; the bargain;

Scene 3d. Village Landscape. Return of the flag; welcome.

Scene 4th. Room at Mrs. Arrington's. Rathbone's prophecy fulfilled.

Scene 5th. Street in Brazoria. The war ended; the oath fulfilled; the stars and stripes once more wave from the staff from which traitors tore it; " Our Flag is There; *Tableau— The Angel of Peace.*

SCENE PLOT.

—o—

ACT I.

Scene 1. Fancy chamber in 4.
"   2. Garden in 1.
"   3. Double scene. two plain rooms in 4.
"   4. Wood in 1.

Scene 5. Street in 4, set house R, 3d E., flag staff C.
"   6. Wood, same as scene 4, in 1.
"   7. Parlor in 3.
"   8. *Tableau*, drop.

ACT II.

Scene 1. Parlor in 3, same as Act 1, Scene 7.
"   2. Tableau.
"   3. Wood in 1.
"   4. Bar-room in 3, bar L. U. E.

Scene 5. Wood in 2.
"   6. Water scene with city in distance in 6. pier L. 4th E., set waters back & front of pier boat ready R. U. E.

ACT III.

Scene 1. Village landscape in 5.
"   2. Wood in 1.
"   3. Landscape in 6.
"   4. Wood in 1.
"   5. Plain Chamber in 3.
"   6. Landscape in 1.

Scene 7. Plain Room in 4.
"   8. *Tableau*.
"   9. Plain room in 4.
" 10. Wood in 1.
" 11. Mountain glen in 6.
" 12. *Tableau*, drop.

ACT IV.

Scene 1. Room in hospital in 5.
"   2. *Tableau*.
"   3. Plain chamber in 3.
"   4. Rocky pass in 4.
"   5. Wood in 1.

Scene 6. Mountain pass in 6.
"   7. Wood in 2.
"   8. Plain chamber in 3.
"   9. Rocky pass in 4.

ACT V.

Scene 1. Dungeon in 4.
"   2. Tableau.
"   3. Landscape in 1.
"   4. Village landscape in 5.
"   5. Fancy chamber in 2.

Scene 6. Street in 4, flag staff C.
"   7. *Tableau*.
"   8. Street in 4.
"   9. *Tableau*, drop.

PROPERTIES.

—o—

ACT I.

SCENE 1st. Handsome set of furniture, nice books on table c.

SCENE 2d. In room R. common table c., papers &c. on table, 5 chairs. In room L. bottles, drinking cups, &c., on bar L. U. E., 3 chairs, lone star flag for Willard, torn U. S. flag ready L., single star for flag for Fred, U. S. flag about 8 feet long.

SCENE 5th. Ballot box on table in doorway of set house R , ballots for men, 8 revolvers, 5 bowie knives.

SCENE 6th. Thunder, lightning and rain.

SCENE 7th. Handsome furniture, easy chair c., pitcher of water and tumbler on table R. c., writing desk, pen, ink, paper, and envelopes in it, on table R. c., pair of scissors for Rosa, lock of hair and nice dagger for Rosa, rifle ready R. handkerchief covered with blood ready R.

ACT II.

SCENE 1st. Same as Act 1st, Scene 7th, anchor for Goddess of Hope, chain 4 or 5 feet long.

SCENE 3d. Bottles and cups on bar L. U. E., newspapers for Capt. Wilson, tin money.

SCENE 4th. Stuffed club for Rathbone, blanket rolled up and tied with piece of small rope 10 or 12 feet long for Fred.

SCENE 5th. Dummie ready L. to throw from pier, tied in blanket just like the one Fred has.

ACT III.

SCENE 1st. Muskets, equipments and U. S. uniforms for soldiers, nice flag on staff for presentation.

SCENE 3d. Camp fire L. U. E., small camp table, and camp stool R., pen, ink and paper on table, written orders for Capt. Allen.

SCENE 5th. Common table and camp stool c., papers, war map, &c., on table, mail bag with letters, papers and plans in it under table.

SCENE 6th. Pie for Dolph.

SCENE 7th. Camp table and 2 stools c., papers and documents on table, blank letters for Fred.

SCENE 8th. Piece of rope 10 or 12 feet long for Willard.

SCENE 9th. Signal color on staff, field glass for Maj. Gen., bomb shells R. & L., cannon and carriage ready L. loaded, blank catridges for soldiers, bass and snare drums, and bugles, R. & L.

ACT IV.

SCENE 1st. Cot R. C., camp stool near it.

SCENE 3d. Halter for Dolph.

SCENE 5th. Camp table and stool R. C., documents on table, bottle and cup on table, newspaper for Willard.

SCENE 7th. Letter for orderly.

ACT V.

SCENE 1st. Old broken chair C., large book for roll book, quill and pair of large wings for Angel.

SCENE 5th. Small flag on pole for Catastrophy, U. S. flag 6 or 8 feet long for Fred.

COSTUMES.

—◊—

JARED WESTON. Texan trowsers, dresssing gown.

FRED WESTON.—*First dress*, nice Texan suit. *Second dress*, any rough suit. *Third dress*, U. S. Uniform, Sergeant. *Fourth dress*, disguised in rebel grey. *Fifth dress*, U. S. Uniform again. *Sixth Dress*, old man disguise. *Seventh dress*, ragged shirt and pants. *Eighth dress*, Maj. in the U. S. Army.

JAMES MOORE.—*First dress*, plain Texan suit. *Second dress*, any rough suit. *Third dress*, U. S. private uniform. *Fourth dress*, Lieutenant's uniform.

CATASTROPHY JACKSON.—*First dress*, as fancy dictates. *Second dress*, U. S. private uniform.

DOLPH.—*First dress*, plain neat suit. *Second dress*, U. S. uniform.

ROBERT WILLARD.—*First dress*, rough Texan suit. *Second dress*, C. S. officer's uniform.

HARRISON RATHBONE.—*First dress*, rough Texan suit. *Second dress*, C. S. officers uniform.

CLAIRE & STARK.—*First dress*, same as Willard. *Second dress* C. S. Privates. *Third dress*, C. S. officers.

CAPT. WILSON & GEO. BENNETT.—*First dress*, any old rough dress. *Second dress*, C. S. Privates.

Ladeis dress as fancy dictates in their respective parts.

SOUTHERN REFUGEES.

———o———

ACT I.   SCENE 1st.

Room at Mrs. Arrington's in 4th groove, well furnished.

Mrs. Arrington R., *Rosa* R. C. *discovered—Mrs. Arrington
reading, Rosa sewing.*

Rosa.   Mother, a gloom I cannot give cause for makes me
sick at heart.

Mrs. A.   I feel as you do, Rosa, but I can assign no reason
for it, except the thought of to-morrow, when the vote of
Texas will be cast for or against secession, and only God
knows what will follow.   Now, more than ever, do I feel your
father's death, for I know how he would vote, were he living.

Rosa.   Why, mother, I cannot see the necessity for breaking
up the country.   Why should they desire to dissolve the Union,
of which, since my childhood I have been so proud?

Mrs. A.   I do not know.   The people are surely crazed, for
most all of them are crying for secession.

Rosa.   Mother, all will not vote for secession; there is one
I know who is brave and strong, who on the morrow will teach
them in the town to do right.

Mrs. A.   Men will not be guided there by ideas of right,
my child; the bowie-knife and revolver will guide the ballot, and
Fred would be reckless to oppose them; his single vote would
avail nothing, and his death would cause a world of harm.

Rosa.   Death!   Would they kill him, mother, for voting
against them?

2

Mrs. A. I do not know. There will certainly be trouble, for if there is any truth in the papers I receive from the North, the bayonets of the Union will be used against the ballots of secession. Let Fred reserve himself for that.

Enter Fred Weston. L. 2 E.

Fred. Good morning, Rosa. Good morning Mrs. Arrington. (*Business of welcome.*)

Rosa. Good morning, Fred.

Mrs. A. Good morning, Fred, what news? (*Fred takes seat* L. C.) Rosa and I were just talking about the election to-morrow. How do you think the vote will be?

Fred. I have been all through the county. and I find but few who are not going to vote to secede. Many, I think, are are opposed to it, but the fear of Willard and his clique drives them to it.

Rosa. Is it true, Fred, that they are going to kill all those who oppose them?

Fred. I do not know. I saw a card on the Court House, stating that those who vote for Yankee rule must do it in the . face of Southern steel. I suppose by " Yankee rule," is meant, in favor of the Union.

Rosa. O, if I were a man !

Fred. If you were, Rosa, what could your single arm do? You could only resist by a vote. and, God giving me strength I intend to do that.

Mrs. A. Be careful Fred ; remember more will be required of you than mere voting.

Fred. I know it, Mrs. Arrington, and I have determined that if Texas leaves the Union I shall go north, for I am convinced war will follow this mad course of the Southern States.

Mrs. A. It seems inevitable. You will excuse me now. my duties call me.

Fred. Certainly.   (*Exit Mrs. A.. R. 3 E.*)

Rosa (*Taking Seat beside Fred.*) Have you seen Harrison Rathbone to-day?

Fred. No. Has he been here?

Rosa. Yes. He was here and poured out a torrent of threats against the Yankees. I reminded him that he was born and lived until a few years since in Connecticut. He said that did not make him an abolitionist, and left muttering vengeance against those who vote for Union to-morrow, and you in particular, as he says you stand between him and myself.

Fred. Poor fool, he is true to his instincts. (*After a pause.*) It is very strange, but there is not one person of northern birth in this section, who is a slave owner, that is not going to vote for secession to-morrow.

Rosa. But there is one Southern man who hates their actions, and who will oppose them. O, Fred, I do feel proud of you.

Fred. Rosa, when strong emotions move the heart, or great dangers surround us, cold etiquette is laid aside, and we stand face to face with no feelings disguised. And as there is a great danger in waiting for us all now, I cannot help feeling that deep, pure love for you that fills my heart. But there is a love higher than that which connects the sexes; a love which forgets all personal considerations when principles are involved; a love which impels the mother to kiss her first born adieu, and send him into the ranks of death; a love which elevates man to the dignity of angels, for it mocks at danger and smiles at death. It is the soul absorbing love of our fatherland and our country's flag. Rosa, that flag is in great danger now, and I feel it my duty to lend my aid to defend it. But I will leave you now. After the election is over, I will call and inform you of the result. (*Exit Fred* L. 2 E.)

· (*Rosa takes seat at table as scene closes.*)

SCENE 2d. *Garden in 1st Groove.*

(*Enter Fred followed by Dolph* L. 1 E.)

Dolph. Mauss Fred, is yeh gwine to de vil'ge to-morrow, shuah?

Fred. Why do you ask, Dolph?

Dolph. Coz, if yeh is, sah, I'd like to go mighty.

Fred. But, why to-morrow, any more than any other day?

Dolph. Wall, Mauss Fred, I dunno. 'Pears tings ain't agoin' right no how. Harrs'n Ratbun hes agoin' to be dar an' he don't like yeh much. I reckon, coz of Miss Rosa, and he tole Sam, his boy, dat hed make yeh squirm yet; an' den dar's Willard, him an' Ratbun goes togedder, and deys gwine to shoot all w'at don't go wid 'em.

Fred. Well, Dolph, supposing all this to be true, and they were going to shoot me, what could you do?

Dolph. Mauss Fred, yeh knows I ain't skeery; yeh know I kin shoot; an' den if deh kills yeh, Mauss, I don't want to lib nohow; dey can shoot me fust. Do let me go Mauss Fred?

Fred. (*Going* R.)   I will see about it in the morning, Dolph.

(*Enter Catastrophy and Jerusha,* R. 1. E.)

Cat.   Hold on a minute, Fred; we've been lookin' arter you all the mornin'.   You see we know there's to be some tearing work done here mighty soon, an' I don't know but a darned few in these diggins that's on the right side, an' I thought Jerusha 'n I'd be too hot for this climate arter they'd got well to work, so we've come to tell you we was goin' back to Aroostuck County, an' start new.   You see we go in for Union; both kinds; the Union of States, and the state of union matrimonial, an' she told me last night that I need'nt look to her for the latter till the fust was a settled fact beyond all peradventur.

Jerusha.   That's just so, squire; any man that can stand by and see our good old flag trampled on and the feathers all pulled out of our Eagle, and not jump right up and show his patriotism. need'nt look in this direction for a wife, anyhow.

Fred.   Then, of course. Catastrophy. you propose to show that you have patriotism enough to defend that old flag we love so well?

Cat.   Patriotism! why, I'm chuck full of it; I was weaned on that air, and the few years I've been working down here for you haint diminished my stock an iota.   We are goin' home, an' I shall see Jerusha all safe. there, then I'm goin' to get my hand into this 'ere row they're kickin' up, an' stick to it till I can march straight across Texas with the American Flag on a pole, an nobody dare to offer it the leastest insult.

Fred.   May success attend you; we may meet in the Northern Army.

Jerusha.   What? are you going too? Why they'd kill you in a minute if they heard you say so.

Fred.   Yes. I shall go; for I cannot stay here and do nothing in this, our country's trial.   If on the morrow Texas votes to secede, I shall immediately start for the first rendezvous of the Northern troops, and join my fate with theirs.

Cat.   Glory! Glory! Glory!   Give us your hand.   How any man in the north, with all the privileges they have had, can have as much as a spoonful of sympathy for the south in this 'ere business, when such sentiments as them are spoke by a southern born, is more than I can see into.   But come along Jerusha, he's got me so much hotter than I was afore, that if I stay here any longer I shall bust, sure, and spill myself all over the cussed confederacy.

Jerusha.   And, Mr. Weston, if you ever hear of his show-ing the white feather during this tantrum, just let me know, an' I'll die an old maid just to spite him.

(*Exit Catastrophy and Jerusha*, R. 1 E.)

Fred.   With an army of men with sentiments like those, the right must triumph.   (*Exit Fred*, R. 1 E.)

Dolph.   Bress de Lor', I hope um may. (*Exit Dolph*, R. 1 E.)

Scene 3d.   *Plain Room in 4.   Partition through middle, making double scene.   Practical door in partition.*

In room R. *common table and five chairs, papers on table. Muth, Watkins, Kent, Smart, and James Moore discovered seated around table.*

In Room L., *bar* L. U. E., *bottles and cups on it, bar-tender behind bar.   Rathbone, Stark, Claire, and loafers discovered, cups in hand, ready to drink.*

Rathbone.   Fel's, I've a toast to give yeh, an' cuss him what don't drink it.

Omnes.   Let's have it Harrs'n. Go ahead old fel. Spit it out, &c.

Rathbone.   Here's success to secession an' a bullet for every feller what casts a ballot agin it. (*All drink.*)

Claire.   I'd like to see the fel' what objects to them 'ere sentiments.

Rathbone.   Well, then, if yeh look out there yeh'll see one ; there comes Fred Weston, an' I'll lay a thousand dollars agin a chaw-ter-backer that he votes agin us ; he's gone plum over to the abolitionists. (*Enter Fred*, L. 2 E.) Hello', Weston ; say, have a drink? Willard's stood a big treat to-day.

Fred.   I thank you, sir, I do not wish to drink. (*Crosses to* R.

Rathbone.   What, not drink success to our cause?

Fred.   I do not recognize you or your cause. (*Fred enters room* R., *business of welcome.*)

Rathbone.   There, I told yeh so. Come let's licker again. (*All go up to bar.*)

Fred.   Mr. Moore, I am glad to see you and the rest of our friends here ; if I mistake not there is a dangerous duty before us to day.

Moore.   True, Mr. Weston, but we must undertake it like men. Willard's party, I understand, swear to shoot every man voting against them. We cannot resist them by force, but by a calm and determined demand for the right of voting as we

choose, I think we can succeed; this threat will deter many
from voting with us, who, I am certain are opposed to disunion.
Let us hope that seeing our course they may take courage and
rally around us.

(*Enter Robert Willard*, L. 2 E.)

Rathbone. Three cheers for Col. Willard.
Omnes. Hurrah! Hurrah! Hurrah! (*All go up to bar
and drink again.*)
Rathbone. Now give us a speech Col., something to rouse
us up; you know just how to do it; come, let's hear from you
about our glorious cause.
Willard. Fel's, I did not come here to day to talk, I came
to act. We are to decide to day, so far as we are concerned,
one of the most important questions ever submitted to any
people—that of being an independent South, or a servile collec-
tion of States 'neath the crushing heel of a despot. Once this
land was governed by true patriots, who had the interests of
the whole country at heart; now the power is wrested from
their keeping and in their places stand, not our rulers, but ty-
rants—men who would rob us of our property, free our slaves,
and place them on an equality with us—with you my country-
men! Are you willing that this thing should be? Will you lie
passive while the chains are being forged to enslave you?
Will you still cling close, like cowards, to what is not the gov-
ernment of your choice?
Omnes. No! Never! &c.
Willard. I rejoice to hear you say no! We hold the power
in our own hands, and woe be to us if we use it not. Already
five of our sister States have gone out, and from their happy
eminence beckon us to follow. Are you ready? are you willing to go?
Omnes. We are! We are!
Willard. Then, if you are, let your votes corroborate your
words. Every slave State will follow us, and we will build us
up a model nation; where the white and the black man will be
protected, and each occupy the position God intended him for;
a nation that all can love, and whose emblem I now show you.
(*Shows the Confederate lone star flag of Texas.*)
Omnes. Hurrah! Hurrah! Hurrah!
Willard. If this is the flag of your choice, haul down from
yonder staff, where now it floats, the flaunting banner of in-
famy, and give the banner of liberty and a united South to the

winds of Texas. (*All rush off* L. *re-enter with U. S. Flag, tear it up, then trample it under feet, leaving it on stage.*)

Willard. And now to the polls and vote, as becomes true Southern men. (*Exeunt* L. *Fred and others in room* R., *pass to room* L. *Fred gets fragments of flag and stands* C. *Moore* R. *of Fred, others on either side of them. Moore speaks as they are entering room* L.

Moore. Friends, we should have expected this ; the mob is perfectly frantic. We are here and cannot escape voting, though it is useless. Let us, then, go forward and do our duty.

Fred. Had I been told yesterday that I would stand by and see this flag torn down and trampled in the dust, I would have pronounced the assertion false ; yet to-day I saw it and did not resist. Here is one star untorn ; let it be to us an emblem of hope. Let all of us here, few though we be, lay our hands on these shreds. (*All lay hands on flag.*) Now swear with me, that come what may, though property be sacrificed and homes surrendered, we will be faithful 'till death to this flag, nor rest 'till it returns again in triumph.

Omnes. I swear ! (*Form picture closed in.*)

SCENE 4th. *Wood in 1st Groove.*

(*Enter Catastrophy and Dolph,* L. 1. E.)

Cat. What in thunder is it ails you, Dolph? What did you get me to come down here for?

Dolph. You see, 'Pastophy, 'peared to me all day dat someting was gwine to happen to Mauss Fred. I couldn't stay up dere to de house any longer ; I want you to go wid me down in the chapperral and wait till Mauss comes ; I'se mighty skeery dat dere's gwine to be trouble.

Cat. What makes you think so?

Dolph. Dunno. 'Pastophy, but I can't help it ; you know dey's gwine to vote to-day, and Mauss Fred he don't vote wid 'em, an' I spects dey'll try to kill him.

Cat. Wall, who do you think'll try it?

Dolph. Dere's Harr'son Rathbun, yeh know he'd like to get Mauss out'r de way mighty well, den he tinks he'll get Miss Rosa.

Cat. Harrison Rathbone ! Now don't you get scared about him ; he's too lazy to do anything that there's work in, an' he'd find a tolerable good job with Fred, an' he knows it. Why, Dolph, Harrison Rathbone is so darned lazy he gets up at midnight to rest his face and hands on the head-board.

Dolph. Dat may be, 'Postophy, but yeh see he's got lots to help him; if he'd only come alone I wouldn't feel so about Mauss Fred, for he'd take care of hisself, but dere's so many ob 'em I 'clair to goodness I's mighty skeery for him.

Cat. Wall, that's so, Dolph; if they come too many at a time he might have more'n he'd want to do. But what are you goin' to do, go down to the town, or wait here for him?

Dolph. I reckon we'd better wait heah till he comes along; I don't tink dey'll hurt him in de town, but when he comes home dey'll play possum in de woods, heah, an' kill him in de dark.

Cat. I guess you're about right, an' we may as well stay 'round here somewheres an' wait for him; I'd like to get my hand into some such row as this just for practice, for I expect I'll have considerable on it to do pooty soon.

Dolph. Dat's so; tings looks mighty bad. Dem fellers is all mad coz dey can't hab eberything dere own way all de time, an' dey's gwine to fight to do it.

Cat. Wall, let 'em fight, they'll get enough on it, I guess, afore they get through with it. Come along; let's go up there (*looking* R.) an' get behind that clump of bushes an' wait for him; I'll get a good cudgel, somewhere, an' be all ready for' em, an' if anybody interferes with his passage home there'll be a CATASTROPHY THERE they don't expect.   (*Exeunt.* R. 1 E.

SCENE 5th.   *Street in 4th Groove.*

Set house R. 3 E., *door open. Table in doorway of house. Flag-pole* C. *Confederate flag on it. Willard, Rathbone, Stark, Claire and mob discovered, business of voting, till enter Fred, Moore, Muth, Watkins, Kent and Smart,* L. 2 E.

Willard. (*Advancing to Fred.*) Here's your ballot.

Fred. (*Takes it and tears it.*) I have one of my own.

Willard. Let me see it. (*Takes and tears it, then to crowd.*) Weston and his party are goin' to vote agin us, who'll stand by and see it done. (*They crowd in front of ballot box, drawing knives, revolvers, &c.*)

Fred. The man who says I am going to vote against my country, or in favor of abolition, LIES. I have negroes, as many as any of you: I am a Southern man by birth and interests, but I owe allegiance to the whole country, and not a part, and for that whole country I am going to vote. (*Starts forward and is met by Rathbone.*)

Rathbone. Don't yeh be too sure of it, yeh votes here when yeh votes right, an' not till then.

Fred. I wish no quarrel with you, but I am determined. I appeal to every man here—for you all know me—did you ever know me to do aught an honest man would blush for? Can you say as much for this wretch, who puts himself forward as the representative of better men? You know I am honest in my actions. Now, Rathbone, stand aside. (*As Fred advances Rathbone opposes him. Fred knocks him down, crosses to* R. *followed by Moore and others, who range themselves up and down stage in front of set house, each drawing revolvers and facing crowd, who fall back* L.) And now, if you oppose us more, you will be met with lead instead of words; we have shown our colors, and you yours; we shall stand by ours 'till death, or the glorious stars and stripes you have this day dishonored waves again over our entire land, without a single star removed, our country undivided. (*Form picture closed in.*)

SCENE 6th. *Wood in 1st Groove.*

Dark stage, thunder storm. Fred enters R. 1 E., *hurries across* L., *shot outside* R. *Fred falls* L. C. *Rathbone, Claire, and one man enters* R. 1 E. *as Fred attempts to rise. Rathbone strikes at him with knife.*

Rathbone. Kill the infernal abolitionist.

(*Dolph and Catastrophy enter* R. 1 E. *Dolph seizes Rathbone by throat, throws him down* L., *choking him. Catastrophy strikes man dead with club, knocks Claire down and holds him there. Fred Rising.*)

Fred. Hold! Dolph. God bless you, my brave men; you have saved me; you have done enough.

Dolph. Bress de Lor', Mauss Fred, yeh's 'live, (*sees blood on Fred's head,*, but yeh's bleedin'. O, do let me finish him; dey'll kill me for what I have done, an' I want to hab someting good to hang for. (*Starts for Rathbone, is stopped by Fred.*)

Fred. No, Dolph, let him be; do not fear; the man who harms you for what you have done, must do it after I am helpless. (*Crosses to Rathbone.*) And you, cringing hound, you did not succeed in your murderous undertaking, thanks to these brave men. I know now who stole our horses, and why they were stolen.

Rathbone. Well, we hid 'em. Willard told us to, and sent us arter you. But you'll pay for this; you'll swing yet for killing that man there.

Fred. You know you lie when you say Willard directed this, it was your own black heart; but as you threaten me I think it prudent to complete this job. (*Puts revolver to his head. Rathbone, frightened, gets over to* R., *Catastrophy gets to* L.)

Rathbone. O, dont, don't, Mr. Weston, it was only a drunken spree, an' we didn't mean to do any harm.

Fred. I was only trying your mettle, Rathbone. I'll leave you now to care for your friend, there, and remember you have struck the first blow, and if we ever meet again with weapons drawn, your lies and supplications will not save you.

Cat. Say, Fred, going to tie 'em, ain't yeh? ain't going to let 'em go back, now?

Fred. No; let them go. I don't think they will follow us any more.   (*Exit Fred, followed by Dolph,* L. 1 E.)

Cat. He says let you go, an' so you can, and you may thank him for gettin' off so easy, for I'd like to send my compliments to the rest of your infernal pack in the same shape HE's got 'em. But get up, an' dust. Hold on! just drop that shooter an' knife. (*They drop knives, &c., Catastrophy gets them.*) I'll take care of these for you, an' give 'em back when I get through with 'em, and now take that carcass betwixt yeh, an' go. I shan't turn my back on yeh just yet, an' if you look sideways till you're two miles from here I'll blow yeh clean through the cussed confederacy (*Rathbone and Claire pick up dead body and exeunt* R. 1 E.) There's a specimen of southern chivalry.   (*Exit* L. 1 E.)

SCENE 7th. *Parlor in 3d Groove.*

Well furnished, easy chair C. *Jared Weston discovered in easy chair, an invalid, Mrs. Weston standing beside him with a glass of water. Table* R. C., *writing desk with pen, ink, paper and envelopes in desk on table; nice lamp on table, lighted, vase of flowers and pitcher of water on table* L. C. *Carrie Weston seated* R. *of table* R. C. *reading. Books on table* L. C.

(*Fred enters* L. 2 E. *Mrs. Weston meets him* C.)

Mrs. W. My boy! My darling boy! they've tried to kill you! I know they tried to kill you, my brave, brave boy. (*Fred. leads her to seat.*)

Fred. Sit down, mother, and I will tell you all about it. O father, if you had seen what I have to-day seen, our flag disgraced as I saw it, you would know with what bitter hate the South are rushing into this mad scheme of secession. In the town we were opposed by Willard, Rathbone, and their gang of cut-throats, who tried to stop our voting, but were unsuccessful, so they followed me home and attacked me unawares, but Dolph and Catastrophy were near and came to my aid before any serious damage was done. I received only a slight wound in my head, and one in my arm; a bath will make all right, again, and I'll go and attend to it now.   (*Exit* R. 3. E.)

Mr. Weston. (*Calling off* L.) Dolph!

Dolph. (*Entering* L. 2 E.) Here I is, Mauss Wesson.

Mrs. Weston. (*Shaking Dolph's hand.*) O, Dolph, how can we ever repay you for the service you have this day rendered us?

Dolph. De good Lor' knows anybody'd a done dat for Mauss Fred; but den I'm sartin glad I was dar.

Mr. Weston. Dolph, you know the danger Fred and yourself are in. I feel it would be neither wise or safe for either of you to remain here another day; you must accompany Fred, and when you get North he will make you free.

Dolph. Why is yeh talking 'bout freedom, Mauss? I haint dun nothing; told Muass Fred so; I doesn't want to be free. I'll go wid him, dough, an' I won't lebe him till I die, praise de Lor'.

Mr. Weston. I want you to get ready now for a long and perilous journey; and you must take my rifle; you will find it hanging up in my room; (*Dolph exits* R. 3 E., *gets rifle, re-enter, crosses. takes Mr. Weston's hand*) you may have to use it, Dolph, and in that event I know you will use it well.

Dolph. Mauss Wesson, I'll take de rifle, an' I'll only use it to help Mauss Fred, I'll stand by him forebcr; I trus' in God to come back agin', for "He tembers de shorn lamb to de storm."

(*Fred enters* R. 3. E., *crosses to Mr. Weston.*)

Fred. There, I am all right, again. Look here, father, this is a star torn from the flag that floated from the staff in front of the Court House; (*shows star*) it was torn down and distroyed by order of Willard; never mind, father I will sew it on the new flag that you and I will hoist on that same staff some day.

Mr. Weston. Fred, you must leave here, and that this very night, for even while I speak Willard may be getting the blood

hounds on your track. If there should be a war—and it looks
like it—I need not advise your course; you will do what I
would were I young again, that is, join the first military organization you meet on the right side.

Fred. I am glad to hear you talk so, for, while coming
home I formed a plan like that you have marked out, and I feel
it will not be many months before you see me back again.

Mr. Weston. It may be long months or even years, my boy,
for the South is strong and armed, but there is a God, and right
will not be overcome.

Fred. I fear that when I am gone Willard's party may be
enraged at my flight, and wreak their spite on you.

Mr. Weston. Do not be alarmed about that; desperate and
unprincipled as I know them to be, I am sure they would not
harm me; they have always treated me with respect.

Fred. True; but if I mistake not, you will find this storm
of secession has changed their natures. Why, even the ladies
to-day seemed drunken with excitement, and blended with the
crowd, displaying the secession badges they wore on their
breasts.

Carrie. (*Crossing to Fred* c.) Fred, how did Frank Stark
vote to-day?

Fred. I do not think Frank Stark is worthy of your love,
my sister. Try and think no more of him.

Carrie. What, brother Fred! do you mean to tell me he
voted for secession? O, no, that cannot be. Two days ago he
promised me he would not.

Fred. I am sorry to pain you more, Carrie, but Stark's was
the hand that pulled down the stars and stripes, and it was he
who helped to trample the flag in the dust. (*During speech
Carrie faints in Fred's arms. he takes her to seat* c. *Mrs.
Weston gets glass of water. Business of bathing her head till
she recovers.*)

Carrie. O, my mother, my brother, do not ask me to believe
this terrible thing. Tell me there is some mistake, Fred.

Fred. I wish I could, Carrie, but it is too true. What!
you Moore?

(*Enter Moore* L. 2 E.)

Moore. Yes, me, and only me. I am the only one of our
party left; they were all waylaid and murdered on their way
home, and I have ridden here to give the alarm; indeed I
feared you were killed. and am glad to find you all right.

Fred. They attempted it, and came near succeeding; but go into the dining room, and after you have had a warm supper we can talk over this matter.

Moore. There is little time for talking. If we wish to continue this life the sooner we are off the better.

Fred. We have been talking it over, and I have decided to go to-night; but go and refresh yourself; why, you are trembling with excitement.   (*Exit Moore* R. 3 E.)

Mrs. Weston. (*Coming down to Fred.*) Fred, I have wholly overlooked your wounds in our other troubles. Why did you not mention it?

Fred. The very fact that I did not shows how trifling they are.

(*Enter Mrs. Arrington and Rosa. Business of Welcome.*)

Mrs. Arrington. You said that you would come and let us hear the news after the election, Fred, and as you did not come we thought something must have happened to you, so we rode over to see.

Fred. I should have come, as I promised, but on my way home I was attacked, and received some slight wounds, which, however, prevented my coming. I am glad you have come here, and you too, Rosa, for I must take leave of you all for a while, but in leaving, it is with the firm belief that I shall soon return in safety.

Rosa. Must you go so soon?

Fred. Yes, Rosa, I feel it would be hazardous to remain here another hour.

Mrs. Arrington. I have relatives in the North, Fred, and I will prepare you some introductions, you may find them useful. (*Goes up to table, writes letters. Fred seats Rosa on sofa* L., *sits beside her.*)

Fred. I must now say good-bye to you, Rosa, for duty calls me away, and when I return it will be to make you mine; keep up a brave heart, and I will write you when I see a chance for you to get my letters.

Rosa. God is too good to part us forever, but be careful, Fred, and remember, that 'mid every danger and trial I am praying for you. And now, before you go, I want that lock of hair you promised me. (*Fred bows his head, and, as she goes to cut one, discovers blood on his head.*) O, Fred, why did you not tell me of this? They came nearer killing you than you would have me know.

Fred. 'Tis nothing but a scratch, take one where there are no blood stains. (*She cuts one.*)

Rosa. I will treasure this more dearly, if possible, than ever, for it grew close to the path of the coward's bullet, and is dyed with the first patriot blood shed in Texas, and in moments of dejection it will nerve my heart and intensify my hatred of those bad men whose acts have torn you from me. And now, in return, please accept this, it may be useful when other weapons are not. (*Gives him nice dagger.*)

Fred. Thanks, Rosa. I will ever wear it about me, and will use it only in my own or my country's defence.

Mrs. Arrington. (*Coming down with letters.*) There, Fred, there are the letters, if you arrive safe at the North they may be of benefit to you.

Fred. Thank you Mrs. Arrington.

(*Enter Moore,* R. 3 E.)

Ah, Moore, all ready are you? well, let's be off. Did you say all those who voted with us are dead?

Moore. Yes. That German named Muth was hung on the Colorado road; Mr. Watkins was shot through the heart, and the others were killed going towards Columbia.

Fred. Poor fellows it was a hard fate, but for every drop of their blood shall they be avenged an hundred fold. But we are losing time. (*Goes up, takes Mr. and Mrs. Weston's hand.*) Father, mother, your blessing (*Kneels for blessing. Music.*) And now good-bye for a while, keep up brave hearts, and all will yet be well. (*Crosses to Mrs. A.*) Mrs. Arrington, good-bye. Carrie, Rosa (*gets* C., *Carrie* R., *Rosa* L., *an arm around each,*) good-bye, God bless you both; and in this dark hour let us hopefully look up to " Him who doeth all things well," trusting Him to direct us and asking His blessing on us SOUTHERN REFUGEES.

Picture. Mr. Weston C. *at back in easy chair with head bowed in hands, Mrs. Weston kneeling beside him. Dolph* L. *at 3* E., *resting on rifle. Moore at* R. 2 E. *Mrs. Arrington* R. C., *seated at table with head bowed down on table. Fred* C. *in front, with Carrie* R. *and Rosa* L. *of him reclining on his breast.*

TABLEAU—UNION REFUGEES.

Slow drop.

ACT II. Scene 1st.

Parlor at Mr. Weston's, same as Act 1st, Scene 7th, well fur-
nished. Mr. Weston discovered in easy chair c.

(*Enter Willard and Rathbone, l. 2 e.*)

Mr. Weston. Gentlemen, what is your pleasure with me?

Willard. We come, sir, armed with the law, to arrest your son, and three of your servants, for the murder and robbery of one of our loyal citizens, and for the attempted murder of others, besides the crime of horse-stealing, which can be proved as well.

Mr. Weston. These are strong charges, sir; but, I rejoice to say, they are wholly without foundation, consequently one is as difficult to prove as the other.

Willard. We shall be better able to judge after the parties are tried, and now I wish to know where we can find them?

Mr. Weston. Indeed, gentlemen, I cannot tell you.

Willard. You mean you will not.

Mr. Weston. I desire to convey no such impression; though I might, with truth, say I would not if I could.

Willard. You must be aware of their whereabouts, and such being the case you shield their crimes from the law' and become a partner in their guilt. But we will not be satisfied with your denial. (*Goes l.*) Boys! come in here, three of you.

(*Enter Claire and two men, l. 2. e.*)

Search the house and see if you can find him. (3 *men exit r. u. e.*) If your son has fled we want no further evidence of his guilt.

Mr. Weston. My son has fled, but he is innocent of the crimes alleged. Last night he was attacked by three armed villains, among them the man who stands beside you. He was wounded, and but for his servants would have been killed.

Rathbone. If that is the truth what did he clar' out for?

Mr. Weston. He left from no fear of a just law and an im-partial judgment, but to avoid the fury of the fanatics, who hate him because he dared to do his duty.

Rathbone. 'Tis a lie, you cussed abolitionist. (*Rathbone starts towards Weston, is stopped by Willard.*)

Willard. Hold! Rathbone, treat him with respect 'till you have some cause for charges against him; he is not the one we are after now.

(Enter Claire and two men, R. U. E.*)*

Claire. We can't find him har', but we found this yere in his room; reckon that means somthin'. *(Shows handkerchief covered with blood.)* ·

Willard. This is further proof of your son's guilt.

Mr. Weston. Do you not know that others who voted for Union were attacked and killed going home, about the same time? You must be aware, too, that all those men had their horses stolen by Rathbone. He acknowledged it to my son, and said you directed it.

Rathbone. No, I didn't. Your son's an abolitionist, an' he voted agin' us, an he called our flag a rag; an' any man what does that should be hung. Willard said so.

Mr. Weston. Mr. Willard did you utter such sentiments to the people?

Willard. I did.

Mr. Weston. *(Rising.)* Then I am as guilty as my son; for had I been able to attend the polls I should certainly have voted as he did.

Rathbone. There; didn't I tell yeh he was an abolitionist? Now, Willard, carry out yeh word, an' have this man put through.

Willard. Mr. Weston, I regret that I must take you to the town, but I am compelled to do so. I shall also continue the search 'till I find your son.

Rathbone. Take the old traitor along! take him along, and string him up if he goes back on us.

(Enter Mrs. Weston and Carrie R. 3 E., *go to Mr. Weston, clinging to him, Mrs. Weston* R., *Carrie* L.*)*

Mrs. Weston. For the sake of Heaven do not move my husband. He is an invalid, and cannot bear it. Take me, my property, my life; but spare him. Oh! by the love you bear your fathers, spare him.

Mr. Weston. Hush, my wife; do not fear; they will not injure me beyond taking me to the village. Mr. Willard, you will permit my daughter to accompany me?

Willard. Certainly! I have no objection.

Carrie. Oh, my poor father, what will become of us? My brother a Southern Refugee; yourself doomed to a Southern prison; while mother and I are left to the mercy of a reckless mob. May God protect us all. (MUSIC No. 11.)

Form picture. Mr. Weston c. *at back, Carrie clinging to him* L., *Mrs. Weston at his* R., *the Soldiers at* R. C. *starting forward, Willard* R. C. *front, Rathbone* L. *pointing off* L.

TABLEAU—HOPE BEYOND THE CLOUDS.

Slow drop.

SCENE 2d.   *Wood in 1st Groove.*

(*Enter Catastrophy and Jerusha,* R. 1 E.)

Cat. Well, Jerusha, this is business ain't it? If we hain't been doin' some pooty tall walking I'll give it up. But I'll tell you what 'tis, I don't feel just right 'bout goin' off in this sorter way, anyhow; it seems kinder sneaking : just as though we was 'fraid. Why, consarn their darned pictures, if they'd only come one at a time I'd lick the hull lot on 'em myself, and settle this thing right up.

Jerusha. Well, Catastrophy, I don't doubt that, eny, but you see they don't come in that way; they "go about like wolves, seekin' whom they may devour," as Mr. Shakespere or somebody else says; so you see you would have too much business at once. But I wish we hadn't got seperated from Mr. Weston and the others, for it feels a tarnal sight more lonesome without them. I wish you could find another horse its too bad that one gin cout; but come, let's hurry up, we'll get there as quick as they do, anyhow. Which way are you goin' now.

Cat. Well, I'm goin' ter cut across lots right down through there. (*pointing* L.) and see if I can't strike the river; and if we do I'll get a boat somehow, then the walking 'll be a darned sight easier. Keep up your courage, Jerusha, we're almost there now.

Jerusha. My courage is clear up. What river is that you're huntin' for Catastrophy?

Cat. The Mississippi. That little place we just skirmished 'round, back there, was Belleville ;—we're in Arkansas now— and that ain't a great ways from the river. I believe. When we get there and get a boat we're all right; we can slip right up the river inter Kentucky; then we can go right along East just as fast as we want to, for they'll be Union there, clear through, I expect.

Jerusha. Well, come along, then, quick. I wish we was there now, for I want you to get a place in the ranks just as

4

soon as you can, and I've made up my mind to stay with the soldiers too. They'll want nusses, and I can do that as well as any of 'em. I'm bound to do my share, somehow, and that's the only way I know of.

Cat. All right; I guess they'll need you, but come along, and lets find the boat.   (*Exeunt*, L. 1 E.)

SCENE 3d.   *Bar room in Tavern, 3d Groove.*

Bar L. U. E.   *Capt. Wilson, Bennett and others seated and standing* L.   *Fred, Moore and Dolph, seated* R.

Capt. Wilson. Boys, did you know ole Jackson went up last night?

Omnes. No!—Yer don't say so!

Capt. W. Sure as shootin'! the boys strung him up, an' I heard they was 'agoin for Morton; I kind'er pity him if they catch him.

Bennett. Serves the dog-goned ole traitor right. I helped boost that cussed long-legged Adams, and I'd do the same for Morton if I had the chance.

Capt. W. Well, he's gone back on us, shuah. Come, let's liquor up. (*All go up and drink but Fred, Moore and Dolph.*) Boys! I'm goin' ter raise a company to fight the Yankees; how many here will join me.

Omnes. I! I! I!

Capt. W. (*To Fred.*) See here, stranger; are you willin' the South should have her rights?

Fred. Indeed I am, and anxious that she should.

Capt. W. An' in case the Yanks should'nt let us have 'em, are you willin' to fight?

Fred. With all my strength.

Capt. W. Then why in thunder don't yeh fall in an' say so?

Fred. Oh, you have no organization, nor do I at present see the necessity for one. But the moment the South is subjected to an act of tyranny I will raise a regiment, and command it myself.

Moore. And I'll be a private in your command.

Dolph. An' I'll go an' cook for yeh.

Capt. W. Come up an' licker, every man, nigger an' all; yeh just the bulliest kind'er boys. (*All go to bar.*)

Fred. Friends, drink my toast. May the arm of the traitor who opposes right wither, and may he who loves not his country, never have a home in the sunny South.

Omnes. Hurrah! Hurrah! Hurrah! (*Drink, and take seats again.*)

Capt. W. See here, boys; here's a paper, if yeh'd like ter hear it I'll read yeh somethin'.

Omnes. Go ahead! Let's har it! etc.

Capt. W. (*Reading.*) Five thousand dollars reward! Brazoria, March 24th, 1861. Shocking murder in Brazoria! The above reward will be given for the body of Fred Weston, the murderer of two of our loyal citizens. He was aided in his bloody work by some one unknown. Said Weston is twenty-five years of age, dark complexion, and wears a black moustache; is about 5 feet 6 inches in height, and has a strong decided way of speaking. All persons harboring or aiding them are subject to arrest and trial as abettors in their offense.

Fred. Where's the man that wants to aid 'em? that's what I want to see. Friends, it was this murder scrape that sent us up here; they came this way, and I reckon we'll bag 'em soon.

Capt. W. Well, if yer want any help, stranger, just call on us.

Fred. Thank you, we may need you.

(*Enter Willard and Rathbone,* L. 2 E.)

Rathbone. Dog-goned if they ain't here.

Fred. (*Fred and Moore draw pistols. Music No. 15.*) There they are! Men seize them; (*men seize Willard and Rathbone;*) there stand the authors of the murder you were just reading about. Away with them to prison, I will be their accuser.

Form Picture. Men holding Willard and Rathbone L., Fred, Moore and Dolph with drawn pistols aimed at them R., Capt. Wilson C., pointing L.. Closed in.

SCENE 4th.   *Wood in 2d Groove.   Dark Stage.*

(*Enter Catastrophy and Jerusha* L. 1 E.)

Jerusha. There's no use talkin', Catastrophy, I'm 'bout played out; I got along fust rate coming up the river. I wish we had kept on; I don't believe but 'twould have been better for us.

Cat. Wall, I don't know but 'twould, but sumthin' kept tellin' me to cut across here, an' here we are. But never mind; there's the Tennessee river, and it wont take me long to borrow another boat, and then we'll stick to it 'till we get clear.

Jerusha. I'll bet we will. I won't leave again, and walk as we have, as long as the boat will float. Are you goin' now, or wait here 'till it gets darker?

Cat. We'll go right along now ; it's as dark as I want it, to find the boat. I should like to hurray once for the American Eagle ; but I guess I wont, I might have too much company here ; but come along, we're losing time. (*Exeunt* R. 1 E.)

(*Enter Willard and Rathbone,* L. 1 E.)

Rathbone. No, don't let's go back, yet ; we'll get him, sure enough, 'bout yere. If that cussed pack of fools back in Smithland had only let us have a chance we'd a nab'd 'em all, instead of going to jail and staying all night, and then we'd a saved traveling three or four 'hundred miles ; but never mind, we're on his trail again, and close on to him, and we'll have him, you bet Lucky for us they had to separate though.

Willard. We'll have to git him soon. if at all, for we're on the Kentucky line, now, and are as likely to meet foes as friends. We must take him unawares, about yere, and make no noise about it ; and as soon as we fix him I want to get back ; I've had a command in the " Rangers " offered me, and I'm going to take it.

Rathbone. All right. I'll go with yer. Hello ! what's that. (*looks off* L.) Thar's a man coming, sure as death ; we'll get back yere and let him pass. I don't feel just like meetin' too many 'round yere.   (*Exeunt* R. 1 E.)

(*Song outside " Wandering Refugee." At close of song, enter Fred* L. 1 E., *blanket rolled and tied with rope under his arm.*)

Fred. Thank God, my journey is almost ended. 'Twould take a weight off my heart to know Moore and Dolph were safe ; they followed so closely upon us we had to separate in order to deceive them. I am so near the loyal States now I hardly think they will trouble me more, and I feel a safety I have not felt for many weary months. I will lie down here and rest me 'till later at night, and then, perhaps, I can get a boat on the river bank, and make the rest of my journey easy. (*Lies down to sleep* C. *Music No.* 14.)

(*Enter* R. 1 E., *Willard and Rathbone. Rathbone goes forward strikes Fred with club.*)

Rathbone. There, I think that has fixed him. I feel well paid for followin' you ; you're out'er the way now, and so perhaps Miss Rosa 'll be a little more docile towards me. What'll we do with him, Willard? 'twont do to leave him here.

Willard. No, we'll tie him up in this blanket, and go throw him off the pier, and if he gets out and comes up the people will think he was drowned. (*Willard and Rathbone busy tying Fred in blanket during speech.*) There it'll be some time before you're seen again, I reckon.

Rathbone. Now come on; we'll finish this job, then Ho! for the sunny South once more. (*Exeunt carrying Fred L. 1 E.*)

SCENE 5th. *Water Scene with distant City 6th Groove.*

Music No. 14. Moonlight. Boat U. E. R. ready to pull on. Catastrophy and Jerusha in boat. Pier L. 4 E. Set water across, front and back of pier.

(*Enter Willard and Rathbone on pier, with Fred. They throw him over between set waters C.*)

Rathbone. There you are; we've made sure work this time. So may all the cussed abolitionists go.
(*Exeunt L. Music No. 15*)

Catastrophy and Jerusha come on R. U. E. in boat. gets C. just as Fred rises, dagger in hand. Catastrophy sees him, catches his hand, takes him by collar with other hand to lift him into boat as drop falls.

ACT III. SCENE 1st.

Landscape in 5th Groove.

Capt. Allen R. and his company formed at back across stage, officers at the front; when scene opens Capt. Allen takes place C. in front of company to read orders. Men at "Parade rest."

(*Villagers enter R. and L.*)

Capt. Allen. You will give your attention to the reading of orders from headquarters. (*Reads.*) Capt. Allen, you will immediately march your company to Logan's Cross Roads, and join the regiment to which you have been assigned—the fourth Kentucky Volunteers. In that regiment you have the honorable position of the Color Company. By order
Major General GEO. H. THOMAS.

Soldiers, I need not say one word to you in regard to your conduct in time of battle; as I have ever found you in times of peace, so I expect to find you in time of action.

(*Enter Grace Holden.* L. 1 E., *with flag.*)

Grace Holden. Capt. Allen and Soldiers; as you are now about to leave us for scenes of battle, it is fitting for us whose prayers and blessings go forth with you—but whose sex compells us to remain at home—to present you with something to remind you of us, even in the midst of battle. What more appropriate gift could we select than this flag, the emblem of our country. In presenting you with this we have no words of counsel to give, as to its protection. WE KNOW that while you have strength to guard it, it will never be lowered in dishonor; and, should you survive to return with it, though it may be tattered, and torn, yet we shall prize it more highly for having passed through the baptism of war, unsullied. And, now, go forth to battle with stout hearts, taking with you our prayers for your safety and speedy return, with Victory emblazoned on your banners, and a lasting peace over our entire land.

Capt. Allen. Ladies: words of mine are inadequate to express the pleasure I feel in receiving this proud emblem as a gift from you. Suffice it, therefore, for me to assure you, that not while we live shall its bright folds be lowered; but in the midst of battle it shall be foremost, and as a beacon light lead us on, and inspire us with thoughts of those who now present it to us. And when we return with it, as God grant we may, may our great republic stand on that broad foundation stone— "one country, one flag." (*Turns to company.*) Attention! shoulder, Arms! Color Sergeant, Advance! (*Color Sergt. advances, takes colors.*) Present, Arms! (*Color Sergt. dips flag three times to Music No. 6.*) About, face! to your post. March! (*Capt. Allen marches the company off* L. U. E. *Music No. 19. Villagers closed in.*)

SCENE 2d. *Wood in 1st Groove.*

(*Enter Fred, Catastrophy and Jerusha.* R. 1 E.)

Cat. Wall! I guess we're pooty nigh onto 'em, now.

Fred. Yes, yonder is a camp of Union Soldiers; our long journey is now ended; we will enter the camp and put on the coat of blue and commence the battle in earnest.

Jersuha. I should think it commenced in earnest, long ago ; we've had to fight and run, all the way from Texas, and I'm glad we're here at last. Let's get in there, quick ; I expect every minute to see some one jump up and try to stop us.

(*Enter Sergeant of Picket,* L. 1 E.)

Sergt. Halt ! who goes there?

Jerusha. O, Lord ! I thought so.

Fred. We are Southern Refugees on our way to some Union camp.

Sergt. I don't know but you're all right ; but my orders were to take all persons found near our picket line into camp.

Cat. Wall, that's just where we want to go : come along.

(*Exeunt Fred, Cat., and Jerusha, Sergt. following* L. 1 E.)

SCENE 3d.   *Landscape in 6th Groove.*

Union Camp.   Muskets stacked up stage.   Camp fire, L. 3 E. *Capt. Allen discovered seated at table on camp stool* R. *Soldiers about stage.   Moore and Dolph near fire* L.

Capt. Allen. Well, boys, enjoy yourselves while you can in camp to-day ; to-night we advance.

(*Enter Sergt. of Picket,* L. 2 E., *to Capt. Allen.*)

Sergt. Captain, we have three prisoners, two men and a woman ; we arrested them near our picket lines. I think, from their appearance and conversation, they are all right ; still, we obeyed our instructions, and have brought them into camp.

Capt. Allen. That's right, Sergeant, bring them here and I will question them. (*Exit Sergt.,* L. 2 E., *immediately re-enter with Fred, Cat. and Jerusha,* L. 2 E. *Moore and Dolph cluster round prisoners, shake hands &c. Business.*)

Dolph. Bress de Lor' ! if dis yere ain't good, to see yer once mor alibe. Mauss Fred, I never 'spected ter see yer more ; clar to goodness, Mauss, I didn't.

Moore. Yes, Fred, we had given you up as lost. After separating at Smithland I came straight here, with hardly any difficulty. Dolph came in three days after. It is now two months since we got here, and we supposed you had been taken and killed.

Fred. No ! thanks to Catastrophy, I am alive and well. I

had a narrow escape, and only the little dagger that Rosa gave me at parting, saved me; but it's too long a story to tell you all now, so I'll finish it by and by. Now we must see the commander and get released, for, you see we are prisoners yet.

Capt. Allen. (*Coming forward.*) No, Fred Weston, you and your friends are free, now. Sergeant, these are more refugees; you can return to your post. (*Exit Sergt.*, L. 2 E.)

Fred. What! Charlie Allen, my old college chum, is this you? This is a pleasure unlooked for. I heard your brother was in the Southern army, and did not know but you were with him.

Capt. Allen. No! Thomas espoused the CAUSE of the South from the first, and joined their RANKS as soon as they began to raise men in Kentucky.

Cat. Say, look here, squire; I want to get into a uniform just as soon as I can. I've been travelling just a year, lacking two weeks, ter git here, and now I want ter turn 'round and go back. I hope we can go back quicker than we come; but I'm going there if it takes the rest of my natral life. I've sot out ter see this thing through, and I'm agoin' ter do it.

Fred. Capt. Allen, this is Catastrophy Jackson, and this, Miss Jerusha Jenkins. They were both in my employ when we left home. He determined to come with me, and fight tor the flag; she has decided to go to a hospital as nurse.

Jerusha. If it hadn't been so unpolite I should have spoke afore, but I don't believe in speaking to strangers without an introduction. But, as Mr. Weston has told you, I want to help some way in this scrape, and Catastrophy says they wouldn't take me as a soldier, so all I can do, as I see, is to go to a hospital as nuss; and so I've made up my mind to do it.

Capt. Allen. No! they do not enlist ladies in the ranks, Miss Jenkins; but they can be full as useful, and perhaps more, in their own way. I will take you to headquarters, and you will be assigned to duty immediately.

Cat. Just show me where there's a uniform; I want to get it on as soon as I can.

Capt. Allen. O, yes; I'll fix you. Come here and sign the enlistment roll, then come with me to the Colonel's, and be sworn in. (*Goes to table* R. *Business of signing.*)

Cat. All right; you'll find me on hand, like a wart.

Fred. Let me sign at the same time, Capt., and go to headquarters with you. I have been inside the Rebel lines, and I have some reliable information to give there that will be useful to our Commanding General. , (*Signs roll.*)

Capt. Allen. All right, Fred ; you shall have the opportunity, and I know he will be glad to hear from you, for our secret service is, as yet, very imperfect. Come, Miss Jenkins.

(*Exit* R. 3 E., *Capt. Allen, followed by Fred, Cat. and Jerusha.*)

Dolph. I! Golly, boys! I feel so good to tink I'se foun' ole Mauss again, I can't hold in no how. I must let it out or bust, shuah ; so hold your breff. (*Does song and dance. After song, assembly beat outside* R., *Orderly falls in, Company, break stacks, shoulder, arms.*)

(*Enter Capt. Allen and Catastrophy,* R. 3 E., *Catastrophy enters ranks, Capt. Allen goes front of Company, reads order.*)

Capt. Allen. (*Reading.*) It is the order of the Commanding General that no soldier be allowed outside of camp ; we are to advance at seven o'clock, and we are now so near the enemy that those outside of camp are liable to be taken prisoners. Captains of companies will see this order obeyed in their respective commands. Per order,

General GEO. H. THOMAS.

The regiment is now forming to advance, let there be no stragglers from this company. (*Marches men off* R. U. E.)

SCENE 4th.   *Wood in 1st Groove.*

(*Enter Willard and four rebel soldiers,* R. 1 E.)

Willard. Now, boys, keep a sharp look-out, or you'll get gobbled by the Yanks before you know it. We're close on to them, now. There's smoke from the fire of one of their Picket posts. Let's get up a little closer ; we may catch some one outside.   (*Exeunt* L. 1 E.)

SCENE 5th.   *Plain Chamber in 3d Groove.*

Major General Commanding Union forces seated at table C., *Fred standing.*

Maj. Gen. I have heard of you through Captain Allen, and I sent for you. I understand you are from Texas ; that you are familiar with the South and its people.

Fred. I am, sir.
5

Maj. Gen. What are your educational advantages? What is your profession? What were you engaged in before the war?

Fred. I was a planter, before the war. I studied engineering at college, in the hope of being able to make the profession useful in Texas.

Maj. Gen. You are just the man we want. It should be the desire of every good man to aid our cause by every means in his power.

Fred. Yes, sir; by every honorable means.

Maj. Gen. Exactly. Now you must know—at least I do—that you can be of more service to your country in another position than that of carrying a musket in the ranks.

Fred. I don't understand you, sir; I prefer to be a private, at least 'till I have EARNED promotion.

Maj. Gen. And there is no more honorable position than a private; but I desire you to aid us in the secret service.

Fred. Do you mean as a spy, sir?

Maj. Gen. Many give the members of the service that name, but in military matters we are all spies. Our object is to learn all about the enemy, and cover our own acts. Every means taken to do so, if successful, is legitimate. I would not hesitate to enter the enemy's lines, feeling sure a great advantage, and consequent saving of life, could be gained by it. Now, are you willing, knowing the dangers, to take a risk for our cause?

Fred. (*After a pause.*) I, am!

Maj. Gen. That is good. Now, are you acquainted with the Eighth Texas—Rangers—I think they call themselves?

Fred. Yes, sir; I am acquainted with nearly all of them. They were raised, mostly, near where I live.

Maj. Gen. An acquaintance with the individuals is some advantage. Do you know Generals Buckner, or Floyd, or Hanson?

Fred. I do not.

Maj. Gen. Perhaps it is as well you do not. Yesterday some of our men captured a mail intended for Buckner; the carrier is here, a prisoner; his name is Trueman. You can take this mail in his place, deliver it, and all the information you can gain relative to his movements, and number of his force, you will report to me.

Fred. I will try it, sir, and do all I can.

Maj. Gen. (*Gives Fred mail.*) You have your instructions, now be as expeditious as possible.   (*Exit Fred, L. 1 E.*)

(*Major General closed in.*)

SCENE 6th.   *Landscape in 1st Groove.*

(*Enter Catastrophy and Dolph,* L. 2 E.)

Cat.   Wall, I don't know but we're gettin' a leetle too fur from camp, Dolph; and I don't see as we're liable to forage much round here, neither.   Let them Johnies go over this ground once more'n 'twill make a grasshopper have tears in his eyes to hop it.

Dolph.   Dats so, ebery time, 'Postophe; tings looks mighty few don't dey?   Look yere; I'se got so much out ob it, dough. (*Takes pie from under coat.*)   Golly, ain't dat nice lookin'? I went in dat ole man's celler, back dere, when you was talking wid him at de front door, and when he said, clar' out! I clar'd out dis pie.

Cat.   Wall, you're a regular out and out Army bummer, you are; to go stealing pies; I wouldn't do that, no how; but be-ins you've got it, I'll help you hide it, Dolph.   Come, let's dis-sect the thing, and see how its built.

(*Business of dividing pie.*)

Dolph.   No, you would'nt steal pie; you'd eat it dough, wouldn't yer.

Cat.   Eat it dough? no I wouldn't eat it 'till 'twas cooked; but come along, let's see what we can find over on that hill there, and then get back to camp.   I think we'll have another fight to-morrer; things look like it.

Dolph.   Well let's hurry up den, for I wants to be dar, shuah.   (*Exeunt,* R. 1 E.)

SCENE 7th.   *Plain Chamber in 4th Groove.*

Table R. C. *covered with papers and documents.   Gen. Buck-ner discovered at* R. *of table.*

(*Enter Lieut. Rathbone,* L. 2 E.,

Rathbone.   General there's a courier with a mail jes' arrived. *Gen. B.*   Show him in here at once.

(*Exit Rathbone* L. 2 E., *re-enter with Fred.*)

Fred.   General, I have brought you the mail from below; there are lots of letters in it from Texas, and I reckon the Ran-gers'll be glad to hear from thar.   Here's one of introduction for me. (*Give letter.*)

Gen. B. (*Business of reading letter.*) This speaks well of you; I will see these are sent to their proper places; you can stay here 'till the return mail is ready.

(*Exit* R. 3 E., *with mail*)

Fred. (*To Rathbone.*) You belong to the Rangers?

Rathbone. Yes! Willard's Company, and they're just the best lot'er men ever got inter this infernal state.

Fred. I have heard them well spoke of. What part of the State did you come from? I ask 'cause I was down thar some four years ago.

Rathbone. You don't say! Well we come pretty much altogether from Brazoria and Fort Bend counties. Was yer ever down in that region, stranger?

Fred. Yes! I had a good time down thar, a huntin', with a young feller I knew at school; his name was Fred Weston. I s'pose he's here with you'uns. I know he was a right squar, sort'r chap, and wouldn't keep out'r such a cause as our'n.

Rathbone. I'm right glad to know you've been in our parts, Mr.——

. *Fred.* Trueman.

Rathbone. Yas, Mr. Trueman; it's next to meetin' an old friend; but your friend Weston turned out bad.

Fred. He did? I'm sorry to hear yer say that.

Rathbone. Well, I was sorry, too, for Fred Weston had many good qualities. He was rich, to, and well educated, and one of the bravest men I ever met; but, fact is, he went agin secession strong. The night of our votin' he met three men, on the way home, who had opposed him during the day, and with the help of his black boy, Dolph, and his Yankee overseer, killed one of the men dead, and wounded the others: one of 'em so bad that he died; the other is now a member of the Rangers.

Fred. Why didn't you'uns string him up? How did he get away?

Rathbone. Just boldness, cussed boldness, Mr. Trueman. There was a reward offered for him, and Willard an' me tracked him to a Town up the river. He was in a tavern thar, with lots of fels, and when we stepped in to get him, dog-goned if he didn't lay the murder on ter we'uns, and afore we had time to say a word they jamed us inter prison, and kept us till mornin'; why, he drank a toast thar plum agin us; 'an them fools didn't see it 'till I explained it to 'em.

Fred. Yeh didn't give him up then, did yeh? You 'uns might a run agin' him afore he got clear, if yeh'd foller'd him, couldn't yeh?

Rathbone. He didn't get clear, arter all. We 'uns foller'd him soon's we got out, and found some of his clothes on the banks of a lake. It seems he met a friend who hid him on an island and the flood come on, and he couldn't get away, and was drowned. So I reckon he's gone to that place where all Yanks have got to go.

Fred. That's so, stranger! AFORE LONG, I RECKON, WE'LL SEE ALL THE YANKS FOLLERIN' IN HIS TRACKS. How many did yeh say yeh had in the Rangers and where are they?

Rathbone. About sixteen hundred, and they are stationed all along from Bowling Green to Columbus, scouting. The Yanks don't know how to scout. We 'uns took some of their men not long ago, and 'twould have made your head swim to see them swing.

Fred. Strung 'em right up, did yeh; that's the way to fix 'em. I don't 'spose there's any danger of the Yanks gettin' this place; got force enough here to hold it?

Rathbone. I don't know 'bout that; 'tween you an' me, I thought we had nigh on to fifty thousand men here; but I heard Pillow's chief of staff say to day that there was only twenty-four thousand including the cavalry.

Fred. Have you any idea of what you 'uns are goin' to do?

Rathbone. Wall, we expect the Yanks 'll attack Bowling Green, then we 'uns 'll join Sydney Johnston and move slap across inter the Yankee country; that's what Willard told me, an' he got it from headquarters.

Fred. Dog-goned if I can keep that feller, Weston out'r my head. I remember his father and sister. His mother, too, was a fine old lady, and if I don't disremember, he used to be attached to a nice gal, thar, a neighbor of his'n, named —— Arington.

Rathbone. Your memory's good, but 'twould be a long story to tell you all. The old man shielded his son, an' was sent to jail, whar' he died; his property was confiscated, and his mothes and sister now live, I believe, with Mrs. Arrington. They're homeless but not friendless. Why! What's wrong, Mr. Trueman? What's wrong? (*Starts to* L. *front.*)

TABLEAU—HOMELESS BUT NOT FRIENDLESS.

Fred. (*Crossing to* R. *front. Picture till after Tableau.*) Nothing! only sometimes I'm taken with a pain in my heart:

it comes sudden, like the blow of a dagger, and then is gone. I've just had a severe stroke, but 'tis past. My long journey and anxiety about the mail have upset me.

(Enter Gen. Buckner, R. 3 E., with mail.)

Gen. B. Here. Mr. Trueman, your return mail is all ready. You must be over cautious with this as there are plans and communications of vital importance within. By no means let them fall into the hands of our enemies, destroy them first.

Fred. I will take good care my enemies do not see them. *(Fred and Rathbone exit, L. 2 E. Gen. B. goes up to table. Closed in.)*

SCENE 8th.   *Wood in 1st Groove.*

(Enter Willard and four rebel soldiers, L. 1 E.)

Willard. We may as well get back to camp now, there's no use scouting around here; our picket lines are so close together they can talk with each other. *(Looking off R.)* Hello! what's this? Halt! Who comes there?

Fred. *(Outside.)* A mail carrier with a pass.

Willard. Advance, with pass.

(Enter Fred, R. 1 E., hands pass. Willard looks at him and starts back.)

Fred. What's the matter, stranger? yer ain't feelin' well are yeh? yer eyes look bad, been drinking hain't yer? drinking's bad for the eyes.

Willard. No, it's nothing, stranger; only you made me think of a friend of mine, when I looked in your eyes, but then he's dead. You looked so much like him then that it started me. Let me see your pass. *(Examines pass, men cluster round Fred.)* Trueman! You ain't Trueman. *(Music No. 15.)* Seize him! boys, he's a spy sure. *(They seize him take disguise off, bind him.)* What! Fred Weston! Now, then, we'll make sure work of it. I thought we had before; we won't fail this time, so string him up, boys. *(They put rope round his neck.)*

Cat. *(Outside.)* Squad, ready! Aim! I'll give yeh one chance to surrender. Lay your guns down and fall into line or we'll blow yeh hull pack inter eternity. Drop 'em quick, or we'll fire. (*They drop arms and fall in line. Enter Catastro-phy*, R. 1 E., *takes rope from Fred and binds them together, call off* R.) Recover, Arms! Forward, march!

(*Enter Dolph*, R. 1 E.)

Dolph. Mauss Fred, we's just in time, agin, want we? You see, Mauss, me and 'Pastophe was up on de hill dar and seed dese rebs go by, so we lay'd low till dey's gone, den you comes along and dey cotch yer, so 'Pastophe says, we'll git him out ob dat, an' I says come along, den, and was jes goin' ter shoot, when he said hold on, we'll took 'em prisoners, an' my golly we got 'em.

Fred. You did it well, and none too soon either. Robert Willard, did I act my own free mind, I'd send you to give an account for all your evil works, before you lett your tracks, but we do not treat prisoners in that way. These men will take you into camp, where you will have the benefit of a trial, something that I don't expect if I fall into your hands. Look sharp after them, now, don't let them get away. I must hurry on with this mail.   (*Exit*, L. 1 E.)

Cut. We'll look arter 'em, you bet; we'll take 'em inter camp. Come. git; we'll take care of yeh. Dolph! cock yer gun and march right behind 'em with me, and if either of 'em turns his head 'round blow him clean through. (*Exit*, L. 1 E.)

SCENE 9th. *Mountain Glen in 6th Groove.*

Maj. Gen. and Staff C. *discovered. Man with signal flag* L. C. *Noise of battle commencing.*

Maj. Gen. (*Looking through field glass.*) They seem to be massing their infantry for a charge. Ah, here comes Weston.

(*Enter Fred*, L. 3 E.)

Well! What success?

Fred. Here is their mail containing their plans. They contemplate a raid into the loyal States.

Maj. Gen. Yes, here is their whole plan of action. Now we can work better. Signal to open fire from our batteries on the right, also to mass our infantry in the center to resist charge. Captain, go and order the fourth Kentucky Volunteers to march out to the right, and get in position to charge on the enemy's flank, after they charge.

(*Exit Capt. of staff*, R. 3 E.)

Fred. General that is my regiment, and with your permission, I will join them.

Maj. Gen. You have it, and I hope you will get through safe. (*Fred exit.* R. 3 E.) Now, the battle is on in earnest. (*Noise constantly on the increase. Maj. Gen. and others gradually working* R.) See that every officer, is at his post, and has his men well in hand. Signal to open fire along our entire line when the enemy charge. (*Exeunt* R.)

Skirmish line firing on the retreat from L. *to* R. *Battle business ad. lib. Shells bursting, &c. Charges and repulse. At last Union men charge across from* R., *met at* C. *by Rebels who charge across from* L., *when bayonets cross Rebels drop on their knees* C. *Form picture. Music No.* 18.

TABLEAU—OUR BANNER VICTORIOUS.

Drop.

ACT IV. SCENE 1st.

Plain Room in 5th Groove.

Music No. 15. *Fred lying on cot* R. C., *Dolph seated in front of cot.*

Fred. (*Waking.*) Dolph! Dolph!

Dolph. Yere. Mauss; Bress de Lor', sing praises to his name, yeh's gwine to lib again.

Fred. Where am I, Dolph? How came I here?

Dolph. Dere, now; stop, Mauss Fred; yeh mustn't say anodder word. Dere, don't move; can't 'low dat, nohow; Doctah says as how yeh must keep quiet, an' may de good angels guard yeh wid dere shaddery wings.

Fred. I feel quite well now. Dolph; but last night I did not think I should ever see a friend in this world again.

Dolph. Not last night, Mauss; why last night yeh was lyin' heah in dis yere bed. as quiet as a lamb. It's more'n two weeks since de battle.

Fred. Two weeks! It cannot be.

Dolph. Dere, dere: not anodder word; yeh's too weak; yeh jes' turn ober an go to sleep. I'se got to go an' 'tend to Mauss Allen now. he had his leg broke in de battle, but he's doin' fust rate now. By an' by I'll tell yeh someting yeh'll like to heah.

Fred. All right. I suppose I've got to mind you. (*Turns away from audience. Dolph starts to go* L. *as Carrie enters,* R. 1 E., *goes towards cot, Dolph goes back to her, comes down with her.*)

Dolph. Sh——; don't make any noise, Miss Carrie. He's all right again. He jes' waked up an' knowed me, an' spoke to me. Bress de Lor', he's all right again.

Carrie. Yes, thank the LORD, for certainly without His aid, brother Fred would never have recovered from his terrible wound; but you go and stay with Captain Allen a little while, and I will sit here and watch Fred.

Dolph. All right, I'll go right along, Miss Carrie.

(*Exit Dolph,* L. 1 E.)

Fred. (*As Carrie turns up stage.*) Carrie, my sister. (*Carrie kneels beside couch, embrace.*)

Carrie. O, Fred, my own brave, noble brother; God knows this moment repays me for all my suffering.

Fred. How came you here, Carrie?

Carrie. (*Sits beside cot.*) I left home to do my share for our cause. There, I dare not have you talk more now; you are not strong enough.

Fred. Well, I won't talk; I'll just listen to you. Now tell me all about your coming here.

Carrie. It's a long story, and I cannot tell you all now. I started for the North, and got as far as Nashville, when Harrison Rathbone met me and had me arrested. On his testimony I was ordered to prison to await my trial, but the Lieutenant into whose charge I was given, found the prison was full and got permission to take me to a private family, named Blake; they were Confederates, but very kind to me. Their son, Lieutenant Charles Blake, of the Fifth Tennessee Cavalry, carried a dozen letters for me, at different times, and left them in post offices where he thought they might reach you.

Fred. Blake—Blake—Fifth Tennessee—with Wheeler, Carrie?

Carrie. Yes.

Fred. It seems like a dream—the suffering of that night, when I laid wounded on the field. I heard a man groan near me, and I crawled to his side; he was wounded and dying. His name was Blake, of the Fifth Tennessee. I gave him a drink of water from my canteen, and he died beside me, asking me to take a message to his friends. Poor fellow! HE was your friend, Carrie.

5

Carrie. He was, indeed.

Fred. Go on, sister; tell me the rest.

Carrie. I remained with the Blakes' during the Spring and Summer. I then came on here, and with all my strength, I have worked to relieve the brave men who have been fighting with you. Dr. Newton gave me charge of Captain Allen, and, learning you were in his company, and asking him about you, he actually fibbed; but then he is such a good, noble fellow I can easily forgive him.

Fred. So, you really think Allen is a good fellow, do you?

Carrie. Dr. Newton said I could take care of you if I would not speak to you, or talk in the room until he gave me permission, and of course I complied.

(*Enter Dolph, L. 1 E.*)

Dolph. Miss Carrie, de Captain wants to see yeh, mighty.

Carrie. Now, Fred, try and sleep again, while I go and attend to the Captain. Dolph will stay here with you. (*Kisses Fred, and exit L. 1 E. Dolph takes seat at head of cot.*)

TABLEAU—SOME OF THOSE WHO SAVED US.

SCENE 2d. *Plain room in 3d Groove.*

(*Enter Catastrophy with arm in sling, and Jerusha, R. 2 E.*)

Jerusha. What makes you in such a tarnal hurry to go? You'd better wait till you get well, and then you can do something; go down there with your arm as it is now, and you'll get in a hospital, and I shant be there to take care of you.

Cat. No, maybe you wouldn't, but somebody else would, and you'd be doin' your duty here, jest the same. There's no use talking, Jerusha, Captain Allen, Mr. Weston—and he's a Captain now—and Dolph, are all goin' to-morrer, and I wont stay behind 'em.

Jerusha. Wall, if you're bound to go, go ahead; I'll get your things all ready for you to night. I tell you it'll be awful lonesome here, arter you're all gone Catastrophy; but then Carrie's goin' to stay; that'll be one comfort; but if you're goin' come along, I've got lot's to do to get you ready.

Cat. Wall, do it, then, just as quick as you can, for I'm goin' to-morrer, sure.   (*Exeunt, L. 2 E.*)

SCENE 3d.   *Rocky Pass in 5th Groove.*

Moore and Dolph disguised, discovered C. *on guard.*

Moore. Easy, Dolph; there's some one coming. (*Looking* L.) Who goes there? Halt!

Frank Stark. (*Outside* L.) A friend with the countersign.

Moore. Advance, friend, with the countersign.

(*Enter Stark,* L. U. E., *gives countersign.*)

That may be good to pass you through some of the lines around here, and it may come handy to us. I'm obliged to you for it; but it ain't good here; lay down your sword; you are a prisoner.

Stark. Why, how is this? I have just left our camp to visit my uncle, who lives just above here.

Dolph. What was yeh gwine up to see yeh uncle fur? Tink he'd be glad to see yeh wid dat unicorn on?

Stark. He, like myself, stands by the South in her struggle for her rights and he will be proud to welcome me as one of her defenders.

Dolph. O, he does, does he? I reckon we'll give him a call, an' see if he won't be proud to have such extinguished visitors as us come to see him. May-be he'll open his heart—an' his cupboard—to us; we'll call on him, sartin shuah; we'll gib him your specs, an' tell him an accident happened to yeh so yeh couldn't come.

Stark. (*To Moore.*) Where is your commanding officer? I desire to see him, and be released, and not stand here to be ridiculed in this way.

Moore. He is but a short distance away, making a disposition of the rest of his command.

Dolph. (*Aside.*) 'Clar to goodness, Mauss'll be glad to see him; he told me if we cotched anybody heah to let him know, an' I'll go an' fotch him. (*To Moore.*) I'll go an' get the cap'n; you can take care ob him till I come back, can't yeh?

Moore. Yes. I've got him safe enough; you go and tell the Captain.   (*Exit Dolph,* R. 3 E.)

Stark. What is the meaning of this? why am I detained here? I am an officer; have a right to go where I like, and I gave you the camp countersign; I did not know we had a picket post here.

Moore.   Our Captain will be here soon, and you can make your explanations to him ; I had orders to arrest any one traveling this road without the proper countersign ; you have'nt got it ; but here is the Captain ; talk to him.

(*Enter Fred, disguised, and Dolph,* R. 3 E.)

Fred.   (*To Stark.*)   It is, perhaps, unnecessary to tell you that you are a prisoner in the hands of Union scouts ; should we be captured in this service, we would expect no mercy, consequently we feel inclined to return none ; your only chance for your life is to answer, truthfully, such questions as I may ask you.

Stark.   I cannot be forced to give any information that will damage the cause of my country, and if you are the brave man you ought to be, to command this expedition, you will do me no wrong for standing by my principles.

Fred.   Might I ask what your PRINCIPLES are?

Stark.   You can, sir.   My principles, as a soldier, are the interests of the Confederacy.

Fred.   Yes, and to promote those interests, you, who now ask life at my hands, would sanction the imprisonment of an aged man ; you would hold him till death came, in mercy, to take him from your cruel grasp ; you would forget every feeling of boasted love for that old man's daughter, and vaunted affection for that old man's son in the hour of their great trouble, and crush them to the earth.

Stark.   Gracious Heavens !   Who are you?

Fred.   I am Fred Weston, of Brazoria.   If you doubt me I can place your finger in the bullet mark of your cowardly assassins.   Yes, Frank Stark, I can show you a fragment of the flag which YOU tore down at Brazoria, and which I am bearing back.   I have a hundred burning evidences in my heart of such as you, and your principles; let me hear no more of them from you ; I might be tempted to degrade myself with your blood.

Stark.   YOU !   FRED WESTON !   AND HERE !   IMPOSSIBLE !   He died long ago, on his way North ; Rathbone told me so, himself.

Fred.   Then Rathbone lied.   (*Throws off disguise.*)   Do YOU DOUBT ME NOW?   Frank Stark, it would have been better for you and your cause if I had died on my way North ; for I am following you with a hatred that will only end with life ; I have much to avenge.   My father, from his grave where your

cruelty sent him, calls on me, and YOU, as ONE of his murder-
ers, must answer.

Stark. Shoot me, Fred Weston, but do not talk thus.
Many things in the past I would change, but as God is my
judge, I was influenced by honest motives. I regret your father's death, and the loss of your property, but it was not my
fault.

Fred. It was the fault of ALL such as you; I care not for
the loss of property, but my mother and sister are homeless,
now, and I am fighting to regain a home for them; but enough
of this, you must be the judge of your own answers to my
questions. Here, Dolph, bring the halter. (*Dolph puts halter
on Stark.*)

Stark. Stop Captain, you've got the dead wood on me this
time. I'll answer your questions. (*Dolph removes halter.*)

Fred. Very well, Where is Willard?

Stark. He is back with the regiment.

Fred. How far from here.

Stark. Not more than a mile.

Fred. What are their intentions.

Stark. They are going on a raid inside the Yankee lines,
to-morrow, and we pushed out to-night so as to give us a good
start in the morning.

Fred. How many men does Willard command?

Stark. About eight hundred.

Fred. Is Rathbone with him?

Stark. He is.

Fred. That will do. Moore you take care of this man and
see that he does not escape. I am going to visit Willard.
Dolph, come with me a little farther, and wait for me.

(*Exit Fred and Dolph,* L. 3 E.)

SCENE 4th. *Wood in 1st Groove.*

(*Enter Catastrophy,* L. 1 E., *intoxicated,*)

Cat. I wonder what Captain Weston would say to see me
now. I'm darned sorry I had to leave him; but when he got
out of the hospital he got a Cap'n's commission and went on
duty in Tennessee, and I had to stay in Captain Allen's company, and come down here to Vicksburg; but it don't make
any difference; I'm bound to put it through anyhow. Hooray!
for the American Eagle, the creetur that flies higher and
squeaks louder than any other bird; Hooray!

(*Enter Bennett*, R. 1 E.)

Bennett. Not quite so much noise here about the American Eagle.

Cut. (*Aside.*) Thunder! there's a reb; I'm in for it now; I'll pretend I'm deaf, and fool him. (*To Bennett.*) Yes, he does make some noise when he's stir'd up, squire.

Bennett. You're a stranger here, I see; what's your business? Your wits seem dull.

Cut. O, yes, Mr. Stranger's business is dull; jes' so. Well whose ain't, these times?

Bennett. I reckon you're a spy.

Cat. Sho! are yeh? How d'ye do Mr. Pry?

Bennett. You're a fool.

Cat. Yes, that's right; keep cool.

Bennett. (*Aside.*) Dog-gone him, I wonder what his name is. (*Aloud.*) You are called —

Cat. Am I? then I guess I'll be goin. (*Starts* L.)

Bennett. (*Seizing him.*) No you don't; you're my prisonr. Come along; I'll soon change your tune, I think.

Cat What! you've got the change to take a drink? Come along, then; I hain't been so dry since Adam was a rag baby. (*Aside.*) I'll go with him; perhaps I may find out something worth knowing.

Bennett. Come, you Yanks are stupid asses.

Cat. Rum and lasses? Yes, jest as soon as anything.

(*Exeunt*, R. 1 E.)

SCENE 5th. *Mountain Pass in 6th Groove.*

Rebel Camp. Arms stacked up stage. Rebels seen about stage smoking, playing cards, &c. Willard seated at table, R., *reading paper. Bottle and drinking cup on table. Pen, ink, paper and documents on table.*

Willard. Well; poor Sydney Johnston is dead. It's too bad, but it can't be helped. We all have to take our chances.

(*Enter Fred with orderly*, L. 2 E.)

Hello! Orderly, who is this?

Fred. I'm Jake Parker, from old Kaintuck; don't yeh know me? (*Willard shakes his head in the negative.*) Wall, I don't know as you would hardly, for I can't say as I ever was mixed up much with you. But I've got suthin' to say to yeh. Will it be safe to speak out afore these men?

Willard. O, yes, speak it out.

Fred. Wall, then, I will. Yeh see I've jist come from tother side, an' thar's a lot'r papers an' letters an' sich. When I come through them Yanks lines, I jist friz onto 'em, for I thought they'd be handy to some of yeh here. (*Gives papers, &c.*)

Willard. (*After looking over letters.*) Yes, these are very important to us; they contain very valuable information. How did you come by them?

Fred. Wall, yeh see, they caught me trying to get through, an' took me up to one of the General's tents, and tried to get sumthin' out'r me, but could'nt, and I was left alone while the Ginral called a man to take me out'r their camp, an' I jist grabed 'em an' brought em here. I come mighty nigh bein' caught agin with these things in my pocket. I swar', it made my har' rise.

Willard. Where did you come from? and where are you going?

Fred. I come from Kaintuck, an' I was tryin' to get to Morgan. Yeh see I haint done much yet in the war, but arter the blasted Yanks took Donelson I couldn't stan' it no longer, an, I made up my mind to go in. (*Fred plays with bottle on table during speech.*)

Willard. Do you ever drink, Mr. Parker?

Fred. Not much, but I'd break an oath to drink with you.

Willard. Help yourself.

Fred. (*After drinking from bottle.*) Thank yeh. But, now, how am I goin' to get to Morgan?

Willard. Have you anything about you to tell who and what you are?

Fred. O, yes; jist read that, (*gives letter,*) an' you'll see I'm all right.

Willard. Yes, this is good. If Sydney Johnston recommends you, you must be all right. You knew he was dead I suppose.

Fred. No! he ain't, is he?

Willard Yes, he was killed a few day ago.

Fred. Wall, that's to bad; dog-goned if I don't want to get at it worse than ever, just to hear that he's dead. I'm goin' to Morgan, and act as scout. I shouldn't be good for much else. What's the best way for me to go?

Willard. You will have to go to Pittsburg landing and around by Tuscumbia. I think you had better be mustered into the service before you start so we can exchange for you if you are captured; I will give you a note to the mustering officer. (*Writes at table.*)

Fred. That's all right. I'll get 'listed, then start right away. I heard some of the boys talking about a raid ych was goin' on to-morrer; are ych goin' my way? if yeh are I can go along with yeh.

Willard. No, we are going right into the enemy's country. It's only a dash with two companies; the rest of my command go another way. There's a certain officer I wish to capture, if possible, besides foraging.

Fred. Wall, I hope you'll catch him.

Willard. I don't doubt but we shall. Here is your note; now go and get mustered in, and then take these documents to Morgan. (*Gives note and documents.*) Be very careful of them.

Fred. All right; I will. I reckon I'll try another drop of this stuff, then be off. (*Drinks.*)

Willard. Look out for yourself now, for you have a risky job to do.

Fred. O, don't you fear for me; I'll get there all right, an' I'll take mighty good care of these papers, too. (*Exit* L. 2 E.)

Closed in.

SCENE 6th.   *Wood in 2d Groove.*

(*Enter Fred and Dolph*, L. 1 E.)

Fred. There, Dolph, you take these papers and go down to Moore, and start immediately for camp. I have read them, and if I get there first I can report their contents.

Dolph. Which way are you gwine, Mauss? I's mighty skeery for yeh, shuah.

Fred. I am going to watch Willard, to see where he is going to strike. You go now as quick as you can, and be sure and get Stark into camp.

Dolph. All right, Mauss; but be keerful. Yeh knows dey'd like mighty well to cotch yeh.   (*Exit Dolph*, R.. 1 E.)

Fred. Now, then, to look after this raid of Willard's; it's unfortunate I could not find out just where they intend to go; but I dared not be too inquisitive. But what troubles me now is the fear that I was recognized by Claire, when coming from their camp. He seemed to eye me very suspiciously, still it may be all imagination. Sh! some one comes, (*looking* L.) it's too late to avoid them. (*Draws revolver.*) Who goes there? Halt! (*Shot outside, Fred falls. Enter,* L. 1 E., *Claire and three Rebel soldiers, bind Fred, and take off disguise.*)

Claire. Thar! blast yeh; I knowed I want mistaken. Dog-goned if yeh didn't fool 'em pooty well in camp, though. But I seed yeh when yeh thought no one was looking. Now get back an' see what they'll say to yeh this time. I reckon they'll string yeh up, or send yeh to Macon. That's just the bulliest town, provided yeh had yeh liberty, to enjoy the sights.

Fred. Well sir, you are at liberty to shoot me, insult me, and send me where you please. May I ask what command is honored by the service of so gallant an officer?

Claire. I'm a Lieutenant in Captain Rathbone's company of the Rangers. I'm one of them fels that'd rather blow the head off'n a cussed Yank than not, so keep a civil tongue in yeh head.

Fred. Yes, there are cowards of that kind, who are always brave in the presence of unarmed men and old women, and I am satisfied you are one of them.

Claire. I had orders to bring yeh back alive if I could, else that speech would be yeh last. Take him along boys; I reckon we'll have a chance to see him stretch hemp now.

(*Exeunt,* L. 1 E.)

SCENE 7th.   *Plain Chamber in 3d Groove.*

General Buckner, R. C., *Catastrophy* C., *George Bennett* L. C., *discovered.*

Bennett. Take off your hat, you're now in the presence of the Major-General.

Cat. Mr. Devil! O, how are ye Mr. Devil? Hope all the little devils are well

Gen. B. What are you doing here? Did you desert?

Cat. No, I didn't come after dirt, I come after butter; hain't had any for a week.

Gen. B. (*Speaking very loud.*) What is your name?

Cat. Catastrophe Jackson, when I'm ter hum.

Gen. B. I see you are one of those Yankees who are always prying into other people's business.

Cat. Well, I'm a Yankee, an' I ain't ashamed ter own it, either, as the feller said when he kissed his gal.

7

Gen. B. Supposing, now you are here, you enlist with us; we will reward you well.

Cat. Now, see here; I took a leetle too much condensed molasses, and this feller caught me; but I'm sober now, an' I'm willin' ter do een' a' most any thing for money, but I can't fight under your flag, cause it's got a " black spot " on it.

Gen. B. You will get double pay with us and have an easy time of it, for you can tell us of the intentions of the army now around Vicksburg.

Cat. Now, hold on! I was allers brought up to know the difference between right an' wrong. I'm chuck full of patriotism; when I'm ter hum I sleep on a mattress stuffed with Eagle's feathers, and the tust tune I ever whistled was "Yankee Doodle," and before I'd betray my country I'd be fried inter slapjacks for the cannibals.

Gen. B. Consider well your refusal; we are making such disposal of our troops outside the city that your supplies will soon be cut off, and Grant will have to surrender. He cannot get re-enforcements.

Cat. Surrender! Grant surrender! He can't find that word in his dictionary; and we got re-enforcements last night.

Gen. B. What! They must have come up the river then; who was the pilot?

Cat. A woman.

Gen. B. A woman! explain; you shall lose nothing by it.

Cat. Wall, yeh see one of the officers' wife—

Gen. B. Yes, yes, go on!

Cat. Wall, don't hurry me; the wife of one of the officers had twins born last night—two of the handsomest little boys you ever seen.

Gen. B. Let us have no more of this foolery, sir.

Cat. I hain't told yeh all, yet. Them twins sleep in the folds of the American Flag, and we tickle 'em with an eagle's feather to make 'em laugh. (*Aside.*) How a feller can lie when he sets out.

(*Enter orderly,* L. 2 E. *with dispatch; gives it to Gen. B.*)

Gen. B. What! Vicksburg surrendered! Orderly, have the assembly beat immediately. (*Exit orderly.*) We must move from here or they'll sweep down upon us, and capture us all.

(*Exit hurriedly,* L. 2 E., *followed by Bennett. Assembly outside* L.

Cat. Have to surrender, will we? that looks like it. He's in such a darned hurry now, he's forgot me. Polite way ter treat visitors, anyhow; but I'll excuse him, and get out of this while I can.   (*Exit,* R. 1 E.)

SCENE 8th.   *Rocky Pass in 4th Groove.*

Frank Stark C. *up stage, Moore* R. *on guard, discovered.*

(*Enter Dolph,* R. 3 E.)

Dolph. (*To Moore.*) Here, Mauss tole me to gib you dese papers an' den we'se to get back to camp, an' fotch him along wid us, (*pointing to Stark,*) jes as soon as we can. .

Music No. 11. *Rebels fire outside,* 6 *charge on* L. *yelling.* 10 *Union Men fire outside* R., *yell and charge, stopping at* R. C. 3 *Rebels fall, others ground arms remaining in position till drop. Moore comes to charge, Stark starts to go* L. *Dolph seizes him, throws him* C. *stands holding him. Picture. Drop.*

ACT V. SCENE 1st.

Dungeon in 4th Groove, dark.

Music No. 9. *Fred discovered seated on old broken stool* C. *Bundle straw* L. C. *Fred nearly starved.*

Fred. The moon shines brightly on the outer world, shedding its rays " alike on the just and the unjust." I wish I could look upon it once more; how beautiful it looks streaming in through yonder grates. I WILL try and see it again. (*Gets on stool* R. U. E. *to look out. Shot outside* R. *Jumps down.*)

Claire. (*outside.*) Get down out'r that; none of yeh Yankee tricks here.

Fred. Is it possible for man to be so fiendish, as to deny a suffering fellow man, even a glance at the moonlight? O, Thou God of mercy and justice, who saw fit for Freedom's sake, that we might better appreciate its worth, to let tens of thousands fathers, and brothers, and sons, die in the cells and

prison-pens of the South—poor starved skeletons—keep down
all feelings of anger and revenge, that rise burning in our
hearts, when we think of this cursed record of a people fighting in Thy name, and asking Thy aid! But, O, keep fresh the
memory of the dead! Remind us when in the world's business
we forget the twin sister of Religion, LIBERTY, of the terrible
sacrifice and suffering by which it was gained. How much
longer must this be? Is there no end? Oh, these thoughts will
drive me mad. It must end soon; God is too good to let such
things be. Soon I'll take my place with those who have gone
to their final muster. I can see them now as they fall in:—
And, now, the Orderly calls the roll. Hark! Don't make any
noise now;—I want to hear him call my name, so I can be
prompt with my answer. Steady,—now;—he's got—almost—
down—to—me.—Sh–Sh–. (*Capt. Allen raises trap* c.)

Capt.   Fred Weston. (*Music No.* 12.)
Fred.   Here! (*Falls senseless.*)

(*Capt. Allen and Dolph enter through trap.*)

Capt.   Fred, speak! come, cheer up again; you are safe
now; we have come to release you. Oh, what a wreck.
What demon's work is this? Death were too good for him.

Dolph.   Mauss Fred, speak once! it's Dolph, come for yeh.
I tried ter come before, but I couldn't Mauss; but I'se here
now and I'll sabe yeh, or die wid yeh.

Capt. (*Kneeling beside Fred.*) I fear we are too late,
Dolph. Hark! There's the boys coming; come Fred, rouse
yourself. (*Song in distance, " Marching through Georgia."
Fred gradually comes to during song.*)

Fred.   That's right, boys, sing and be happy; I am, now.
If you had been in that terrible place with me, you'd sing glad
songs on your deliverance. Captain are you here too? I didn't
see you before; Isn't it nice, after so long a time in prison, to
meet our comrades again? But you was not at the roll call;
I didn't see you there, and I did not hear your name called.
But you are here now. (*Rising sees Dolph.*) What! Dolph!
you too! Are they all here? Thank God! I knew it would
end soon. I don't fear Willard now; he can't harm me more;
but it was cruel to starve me so.

Dolph.   You stay wid him Mauss Allen; I'll find him. I
know now who done dis. Mauss Fred if you die here he shall
go wid yeh.   (*Exit*, R. 3 E.)

Capt.   No, Fred, he cannot harm you now, you are with

friends who will save you. Come, cheer up, you'll come out
all right again.

Fred. What's this?—Where am I?—In prison again? O,
that's too bad; after finding my old Capt. and Dolph.

Capt. We are here now, Fred. See don't you know me?

Fred. (*Business of waking.*) Yes! Thank Heaven; it is
not all a dream; I know you Captain, now. But how did you
get here.

Capt. Sherman has started to march through Georgia, we
got here to-night. I found out, by some prisoners we captured,
that you were here, and in searching through the prison for
you saw that trap door; curiosity led us to open it, and we
found you just as you fell senseless.

Fred. But, where is Dolph, now?

Dolph. (*Outside.*) Here, Mauss Fred. (*Enter* R. 3 E.
dragging Willard, dead, drops him C.) Couldn't help it; he
tried to shoot me fust, and so I jes' fired to sabe myself. I
wanted to bring him alibe, so Mauss Fred could see him die;
for I tink it would do him good.

Fred. No, Dolph, I did not wish to see it. Although I
have suffered much from him, still, as he lays there dead, I
bear him no malice, and forgive him even as I hope to be for-
given; and, as I now leave these gloomy walls, let me utter
the hope that he has gone to his maker; and when the final
roll shall be called may he be in line and ready to answer—
HERE.   *Form Picture.*

TABLEAU—FINAL ROLL CALL.

Closed in.

SCENE 2d.   *Landscape in 1st Groove.*

(*Enter Catastrophy and Jerusha,* R. 1 E.)

Cat. Yes, that's what I say; let's go right down there
again. Mr. Weston'll want you just as much as ever, and so
shall I, and more too, for you've stuck to it well; you've done
your duty like a man, and I'm proud of yer. Now I tell yer
what, I'm going ter git a flag an' put it on a pole, an' when we
git ter the line of Texas, we'll walk all the way home. I'll
carry the flag and whistle "Yankee Doodle," you can help out
on the chorus. I said I'd carry it across Texas, an' I will, an'
I'd like to see ther feller what wants ter insult it.

Jerusha. Me too! An insult was never given to that flag
yet, an' went unavenged. You've got to go up with the company, hain't you, to get dismissed?

Cat. Yes, an' I'm sorry Maj. Weston,—He's a Major now, Jerusha.—I'm sorry he can't be there. He sent word to Capt. Allen that he could not possibly come; he's a provost Marshal somewhere, I forgot where he said, an' he's just finishing up the business there and can't leave. He says he's gettin' along first rate since he left the prison. Capt. Allen told me he did look awful, starved almost to death.

Jerusha. I heard him when he told Carrie about it. She's goin' to stay 'till the Company is dismissed, an' then he's going down home with her, an' they are goin' to be married the same day that Fred an' Rosa are.

Cat. Good! I'm glad of that, for Capt. Allen is a fust rate man. Carrie has worked hard, too, during this war, and she's every way worthy of him.

Jerusha. That's so! There ain't a great many done more than she has.

Cat. See here, Jerusha, I'v got an idea. We might just as well get hitched up the same time the rest do; perhaps it'll be cheaper for us, then; everything'll be all there ready you know. What do you say?

Jerusha. Wall, I say this; you've stuck to the Union well, an' I'll stick to you just the same. (*Assembly beat outside* L.) There goes the drum, now you've got to go. I'm goin' up an' see them.

Cat. That's right, come along.   (*Exeunt,* L. 1 E.)

SCENE 3d. *Landscape in 5th Groove, same as Act 3, Scene 1st.*

Capt. Allen with his Company at back of stage, formed for dress parade, open ranks, Lieutenants in front, Moore a Lieutenant. When scene opens, Capt. Allen goes C. *in front. Business of drill. Villagers,* R. & L. *Grace Holden,* L.

Capt. Allen. Miss Holden, and Ladies: you well remember when we left our homes to march to scenes of conflict. At that time you presented us with a beautiful flag, as a token from you, that, while in camp, on the march, or in the battle charge, we might have something to remind us of those we left behind. In accepting that flag we imposed upon ourselves the duty of defending it; to guard it faithfully, and, if we survived, to bear it back to you in triumph. Our record during the struggle will show how that duty has been performed. We have brought it back to you, but you would hardly recognize it; its bright folds have faded, it is tattered and torn, but it is as pure and spotless as when we received it from you. Allow me now, in behalf of my command, to confide it to your keeping again; and with it, the thanks and kindest wishes of those who have been led on to victory under it.

Grace Holden. Captain Allen, and Soldiers: I felt greatly honored when I was chosen by the Ladies to present you this flag. I feel more than honored now, to receive it back again. True, it is faded and torn; its bright colors are gone; still, as we look upon it to day, it seems better and handsomer than ever before; for it bears the scars of many hard fought battles; it has carried freedom all over our land; and, as we now lay it aside, it is with the heartfelt prayer that you may never again be called upon to rally to its protection, but, that Liberty and Peace, may henceforth be yours. In conclusion, let me say, we give you that welcome home you have so nobly earned, we have also prepared a pleasant entertainment for you all, this evening, where you will—we hope—forget, for the first time for years, the duties and dangers of a soldier's life.

Capt. Allen brings Company to close order, stack arms, break ranks. Business of welcome to all as scene closes.

SCENE 4th.   *Fancy Chamber in 2d Groove.*

(*Enter Mrs. Arrington and Rosa,* R. 2 E.)

Mrs. A. I don't know how it was done, but I believe he was at work on some kind of a torpedo, when it exploded, destroying both of his eyes.

(*Enter Carrie Weston,* R. 2 E.)

Carrie. Good morning.

Mrs. A. and Rosa. Good morning, Carrie. (*Business of welcome.*)

Carrie. I just saw as I came in the most pitiful looking sight I ever witnessed, and I hope never to see such an one again.

Rosa. What was it, Carrie?

Carrie. I met a man—led by a black boy—with such a disfigured face I should hardly know it was a human being.

Mrs. A. Did you recognize him as any one you ever saw before?

Carrie. No! do you know who he is? Have you ever seen him?

Rosa. Yes, we were just speaking of him as you came in. He is Harrison Rathbone. He is perfectly destitute, and lives only by the charity of those to whom, for years, he has been a bitter enemy.

Carrie. His family have suffered much by this war. His father, you know, sold everything he had to purchase our place at the time it was seized by the rebels; of course the title he gave to the purchaser of his property, holds good. Unfortunately the confederacy,—as they called it—could not give so secure a title to him, and Fred, has just recovered it all back, and he is, to day, as poor and destitute as his son.

Rosa. God's ways are past our finding out. Nearly four years ago, Harrison Rathbone, vain, weak and boastful, was sitting in this very room, telling Mother and I, that Fred was drowned; that he knew it to be true. He then made a proposition for my hand, which I spurned, and ordered him from the house. I never shall forget how he raved; he cursed us all here, called us Yankee abolitionists, and used every epithet he could command; he cursed the union and the flag; and when I told him that the flag of the union would yet float from the place from which men like him in feeling but better in heart had torn it he said, " So help me God, these eyes will be blasted before ever they rest on Fred Weston here." They never will; but, thank God, Fred Weston lives, and to day will raise the old flag there.

Mrs. A. Yes, and we must get ready to go and see them raise it. Come into the other room, Carrie, and wait for us, and we will go to the town together.   (*Exeunt,* L. 1 E.)

SCENE 5th. *Street in 4th Groove, same as Act* 1, *Scene 5th.*

Music No. 3. Flag Staff, c. *Soldiers ranged up and down stage* L., *Moore in command. Villagers on* R. *Enter Catastrophy and Jerusha* L. U. E., *Catastrophy whistling* " *Yankee Doodle.*"

Cat. How'd do everybody? Glad to see yeh all alive an' kickin'. I reckon by the looks we're just in time for muster. Goin' to hoist 'er up agin to day are yeh? Wall, that's bunkum. You see what made us so late was, we've walked all the way from the Texas line. When we went away from here, I

said I wouldn't give her up 'till I could carry this flag across
Texas without its bein' insulted. Wall, Jerusha an' I, we've
brought it so far, but one feller on the way thought he was
smart, and said so; but he don't think so now; I took the
starch out'r him so darned quick he didn't know when I began.
(*Looking* R.) Hullo! there comes Maj. Weston and the Gals,
and Capt. Allen and Dolph, gewhitiker, this's good's a huskin'.

(*Enter,* R. U. E., *Fred, Rosa, Mrs. A., Mrs. W. Capt. Allen,
Carrie and Dolph, range themselves at back, Fred* C.
Fred brings flag with him.)

Moore. Attention! Shoulder, Arms! Present, Arms!
Fred. Shoulder, Arms! Order, Arms! Parade, Rest.
(*To Catastrophy and Jerusha.*) Welcome, my friends. I am
glad you got here to day. I was afraid you would be late.
Cat. Wall, we did come pooty nigh it; but we're here.
Glad to see yeh lookin' so well.
Jerusha. And so am I. But let's git cout of the way here,
and let'em go ahead; this is the last act of the war, and let's
have it over with. I've seen enough. There's one thing Catastrophy wanted me to ask you, Mr. Weston, an' I might as
well do it now, that is, if you're willin' him an' I should be
married at your house the same time you an' Rosa, an' Capt.
Allen an' Carrie are? We can't rig up quite so nice as you
folks will, but for the last few years we haint been any disgrace
to the uniform we wore, an' we wont be there.
Fred. Indeed you have not; you have honored it; and I
shall think it an honor to my house to have such noble hearts
united within it.
Cat. That settles it; don't say any more; we'll do it.
Dolph. Bress de Lor', ebery ting has come all squar' agin.
Fred. Yes, it is all square again; we have this one duty,
only, to do, raise this flag. Although we were mustered out of
service some time ago, yet it is just and fitting that we appear
at this time, in the uniform we have won a right to wear; the
same we wore while fighting to bring this flag back here. On
this blue field I have, with my own hand, placed an extra star:
one from the flag torn from this staff by the hand of traitors;
you all know its history; know that a little band of us swore
never to rest, until we brought it back in triumph, I carried
that star with me North; it was in my breast at Somerset,
Donaldson and Shiloh. A rebel bullet pierced it 'ere it en-
tered my body, where now it is lodged. Of the men who

8

hauled down that flag, but few are left. Willard met a just
doom at the hands of Dolph. Stark sleeps at Johnson's Island,
where he died, a prisoner in our hands. Claire lies on the bank
of White Oak River. Rathbone still lives a frightful wreck.
Others sleep on many a battle field; a few wounded survivors,
and others, homeless and friendless, are left. God knows I
would, and will, do all in my power to make them happy under
the flag they fought to dishonor. I did not intend to say so
much, but my heart is full of the memories of the past, and the
pleasant surroundings of the present. Let us now run up the
flag and give three hearty cheers as it goes up. (*To Soldiers.*)
Attention! Shoulder, Arms! Present, Arms! (*Runs flag
up, all cheer.*) Shoulder, Arms! Order, Arms!

Song, "*Our Flag is There*." *After song*,

TABLEAU—THE ANGEL OF PEACE.

Fred. Our Drama's ended; "Our Flag is there." Long and
hard did we labor to bring it back, and severe were the suffer-
ings of the SOUTHERN REFUGEES. When, in after years,
around our firesides we tell of those, who, at the trumpet call,
left home, and all that was dear to them behind, and went forth
to battle for the right; how, through long years of adversity,
they toiled on, hoping, almost against hope, faltered not when
overcome by defeat, and returned, only when the battle was
won, let us not forget, that, while the North was pouring
forth her patriots, resolved to do or die, there were SOME LOYAL
HEARTS in THE SOUTH DURING THE WAR.

Villagers.   *Moore, Soldiers,*
Dolph, R. *Mrs. W., Capt. Allen and Carrie*, R. C. *Fred and*
Rosa, C. *Mrs. A.*, L. C. *Catastrophy and Jerusha*. L.